DUCHESS RISING

Book Two of the Seven Realms of Ar'rothi

ALISON NAOMI HOLT

Denabi Publishing

ACKNOWLEDGMENTS

Cover created by Vicki Adrian of
All Cover Book Designs

LINK TO GLOSSARY

There are many characters in this series, and if you ever find yourself needing a character's name, I have included a Glossary at the end of the book that you can easily access HERE.

**REMEMBER TO BOOKMARK YOUR PLACE IN THE BOOK SO YOU CAN RETURN AFTER VIEWING THE GLOSSARY

CHAPTER 1

The Black Panther silently stalked the child who was methodically sliding forward on her belly. The great Cat scrutinized each of the girl's movements down to the last twitch of her smallest finger.

The sounds of stone sharpening steel, metal spoons clanking against cook pots and quiet conversations surrounded the still form as she waited for the exact time where she could inch one hand forward, possibly accompanied by a knee sliding silently through the mud.

When the muscles of her right arm tensed in anticipation, the Panther whispered into the girl's mind. *To your right. Do you see the man moving into the brush to relieve himself? Wait for his return.*

Kaiti slowly released her breath and closed her eyes. This was something her Spirit Guide had taught her to do whenever she found herself hiding in the midst of an enemy encampment.

Too often, the whites of your eyes give you away. If you stare at an enemy while you wait, your prey feels your presence, even if he never sees you. Still your heart and mind while you mark time.

When she heard the man return to his tent, she opened her eyes. Her target was still twenty paces away, seated on a log next to his son, who was methodically sharpening the thirteen-inch dirk he held in his lap. The fire in front of them crackled, sending off wisps of light that created shadows behind them where assassins could lie in wait.

The child edged to her right, using the long shadow stretching out behind the king to mask her movement. Members of the Imperial Guard stood sentinel, their swords buckled at the ready and their shields held stiffly by their sides.

When Kaiti came to within striking distance, the Panther cautioned her, *Move quickly and be sure of your thrust.*

The killing strike was quick and sure. The second the tip of the stick punched into the back of the king's gambeson, he leapt to his feet, sword drawn and ready for battle.

The Guards reacted also, instantly surrounding their liege and his attacker.

The prince jumped to his feet, the dirk he'd been sharpening now held ready to defend his father.

Kaiti froze. Although she didn't fully understand the Anacafrian language, she'd been told to expect this reaction and had been drilled on the exact response she should have when the king and his guards turned on her.

"Your Majesty! Hold!"

The king swung around to face the Lord Commander of his Imperial Guard. "Jathez! What is the meaning of this?" He turned and bellowed for his cousin. "Bree!"

Jathez calmly walked forward and pushed the tip of the king's sword away from the child's throat. "Your Majesty, as you know, Queen Desdamea has sent assassins into Anacafria. I have increased the amount of training for the Royal Guards, and as such, I asked the Duchess Makena if her daughter would attempt to assassinate you in order to test your guard's abilities." He glared dangerously at his men. "Obviously more training is in order."

The king sheathed his sword, his irritation showing as he rammed the blade down into his scabbard. "A child! You used a child to assassinate me? I could have killed her!"

Duchess Aurelia "Bree" Makena stepped out of the shadows and walked up to him. "A child whom we've discovered is a better tracker and hunter than most of the men and women in your royal retinue of spies." She smiled wickedly. "Besides, her Spirit Guide would have bitten off your arm before you could have done any real harm."

The king and his men nervously glanced around the encampment; none really believing in Spirit Guides, but spooked by their mention, nonetheless.

The prince, on the other hand, excitedly squinted into the shadows hoping to catch a glimpse of Kaiti's Guide, the Black Panther, Denabi.

To the Anacafrians, up until a few months ago, Spirit Guides were a myth, a fable made up by the Shona as part of their mystical beliefs.

When the Duchess Makena had been wounded in battle and brought to her castle in Orinshire, King Leopold, his Queen, Arabetha and many from the king's retinue rode from Cafria to Danforth to hold vigil while the healers fought to keep her alive.

During that time, Bree's friend and healer, Becca Solárin, regaled the court with the stories of what became known as The Battle of the Seven Realms, where Anacafrians and Shona alike fought beside their Spirit Guides to stop the incursion of the black Teivaiedin from Morgrad's Realm.

The king angrily waved his hand, palm down, silently telling his guards to resume their posts.

The biggest guard, Rocca Andresen, walked behind Kaiti and stationed himself in the gap she'd used to infiltrate the king's defenses.

Jathez watched him set himself in the guard position; legs shoulder width apart, back to the fire. "Too little, too late, Rocca."

Rocca turned and fixed somber eyes on his commander, addressing him with the dialect peculiar to the people of the Iron-moor Forests in the Northern regions of Bree's Duchy of Danforth. "T' other's meight seh t' bairn played 'em for fools. Not uz. I'm not ta chuffed ta learn fra t' bairn, Commanda. I'll learn fra anyone who'll 'elp wee protect t' king." He looked down on Kaiti then. "If anyone gives theur grief for lakin' 'em eur fools, theur cum finn' owd Rocca. I'll set 'em straeight."

Very few people outside of the Ironmoor Forests understood their jargon. The people of that region were strong and hearty, and many served in the various divisions of the king's armies. Jathez preferred to use Ironmoor's men and women in the Imperial Guards because they were fiercely loyal and trained many candlemarks after most soldiers quit for the day.

Ten-year-old Prince Darius pursed his lips trying to decipher Rocca's words. He finally gave up. With brow furrowed, he turned to look at his father who chuckled when he saw the boy's comical expression.

The king smiled at the big guard. "I don't think my son quite understood you, Rocca." To his son, he said, "He just told Kaiti that he didn't care if she showed him to be a fool. He's determined to learn from what she just did, and if anyone bothers her because she broke through their defenses, she's to come to him and he'll have a word or two with them."

Darius nodded solemnly. He took the duties of crown prince very seriously, and one of the tasks he'd set for himself was learning all twelve dialects spoken throughout his father's kingdom. He glanced at Kaiti. "She won't understand what he said, but I'll remember to ask Becca to translate the next time she's here."

He turned his attention back to Rocca and spoke with all the dignity a ten-year-old could muster. "I want to know if anyone bothers her. She is under my protection."

Rocca faced the boy, then dipped his head in acknowledgement. "I'll inform theur, thy 'ighness, bur t' 'uns whoa should be worried is t' 'un whoa bothers 'a. She's eur 'ellion, 'a' 'un is." He regarded Kaiti a minute, then once more returned to his guard position.

Unsure about why everyone kept looking at her, Kaiti walked over and stood next to Bree, who laid her arm across the girl's shoulders.

The king turned and settled back onto the log with Darius taking his place beside him. "While you're here, Bree, Jathez, come sit by the fire a while. There's a lot we need to discuss about Organdy and something else I have to get off my mind."

The king's squire, Eavan, ducked inside the pavilion, brought out two stools and set them near the fire. She smiled and winked at Kaiti, then returned to the pad she'd been sitting on before the child stabbed the king. She patted the spot beside her, inviting Kaiti to come sit next to her while the others sat around the fire and talked.

Kaiti glanced up at Bree, who nodded her approval. When Kaiti saw that Eavan was cleaning and oiling the king's leather, she quickly ran to Bree's tent to retrieve a bridle before joining Eavan on her blanket. Since Eavan didn't speak Shona and Kaiti didn't understand Anacafrian, the two of them worked in companionable silence as they listened to the king's conversation.

Seeing that the lessons were over for the day, Kaiti's Spirit Guide, Denabi, quietly faded from sight.

Bree watched her disappear before turning to Jathez. "So, Desdamea's sent her Sabers after Leo. Does she honestly think her assassins can penetrate this far into Anacafria?"

Jathez motioned for Bree to take one of the stools, which she did. He pulled his black cloak in tighter around his muscular frame and lowered himself down onto the other.

Bree still suffered from stabbing headaches as a result of being clubbed unconscious with a stone mallet during their battle with the Teivaiedin. She subconsciously rubbed the back of her head to ease some of the pain.

Jathez sympathized as she applied pressure to a spot just above her neck. He'd had his fair share of concussions and knew first hand how bad the pain could be. "Not just the king. Do you know Ruthok, the commander of the Fourth Contingent of the Archers?" He paused, waiting to see if Bree knew the man he was talking about.

Bree let her hand drop to her lap. "I know him well. He served as the assistant armorer at Orinshire before he joined the Archers. He's a good man."

Jathez raised bushy eyebrows. "I didn't know he was an armorer. That explains how he knew the difference between a trench knife and the saluri skivvers the Sabers use during close-in assassinations. He and his squad captured a Saber coming off a ship at Port Emnal, just south of Moorhaven. The idiot wore his skivver under his cloak and a gusting wind blew the cloak open far enough for Ruthok to get a chance look at the blade. It took a little...convincing, but the Saber eventually admitted that Queen Desdamea sent several assassins, like himself, after the king and queen, the prince, and you, as well, Duchess."

Prince Darius, who was just now learning that he and his mother were targets, spoke up. "Why would an assassin tell Ruthok anything? How do you know what he said is true?" The slight tremor in his voice revealed just how much the news from Jathez unnerved him.

The king placed his hand on the prince's knee. "Now, Son, there's nothing to fear. We've the best Imperial Guards of any of the surrounding kingdoms and they'll not get within a hundred leagues of here."

Darius studied the men and women standing guard around the royal tents. "But how do you know she's targeted us? Why would an assassin tell Ruthok who his target is?"

The three adults in the group exchanged glances. Jathez opened his mouth to speak but the king held up a hand to silence him. "There are many ways to make a man or woman speak, Darius. None of them fit for the ears of a ten-year-old boy. Suffice to say, we trust the information Jathez has been able to gather, and we've taken the appropriate steps to protect everyone." He ruffled the boy's hair. "Including you. But I want you to be on guard—more so than usual. If you see something that just doesn't sit right with you, tell whatever guard is assigned to you at the time."

Once again, the prince studied his guards. Nordin and Kalsik had been chosen to protect him during the long ride back to King's City with his father. His mother, the queen, had left a week earlier to attend the wedding of her best friend, and he was ecstatic to learn he'd be traveling with the king.

Nordin stood guard at the moment. Darius watched him while the others continued on the topic of the Orgundian queen. The dark-skinned guard stood straight and tall, his overly muscled arms almost blending with the gambeson dyed the black and jade of Darius' heraldic device. Like the prince's older cousin, Bree, Nordin wore a bandolier of throwing knives crossed in front of his chest. He also carried a long sword, and a shield bearing Darius' insignia of a Jade Silvermoor Leopard Rampant.

The prince's father didn't believe in actual Spirit Guides, but he was fond of telling his son about the day Taklishim, the most revered shaman of the Shona tribes, had come to pay the newborn prince a visit. Taklishim had held Darius in his arms and proclaimed to the assembled courtiers and advisors that his Spirit Guide was one of the famed white Silvermoor Leopards.

Whenever the healer, Becca Solárin, was at the castle, Darius wouldn't let her rest until she once again explained about the Spirit Guides and how he could learn to see and hear *his* Leopard. He glanced around now, wishing his Guide would appear and teach him what he needed to know about being a brave and noble soldier and, someday, a strong and wise ruler like his father.

King Leopold noticed him and misinterpreted the action. "There really is no need to worry, son. You are well protected."

Darius glanced down at the fire. He saw no reason to explain what he'd actually been looking for. Even though Bree and Becca told the king about their experiences with the Guides and the Teivaiedin, his father still didn't believe. He might never come to acknowledge their existence, but that didn't keep Darius from expecting to see a Silvermoor Leopard come strolling out of the darkness some starlit night.

He stared out at the surrounding landscape. The soft yellow glow of fifty or more cook fires hovered over their encampment. This was a soldier's bivouac, something very different from the camps he'd been in with his parents when they'd been on one of their summer holidays. Tents were picketed in ten consecutive, concentric circles around the king. If a spy studied the encampment from the top of the tallest Runyon Tree, the formation would look like a giant target with Leopold's pavilion a bullseye in the middle.

Darius glanced up at his father's golden pennant fluttering in the breeze. Taklishim said that his father's Spirit Guide was a Therian Mountain Goat, one of the hardiest and most steadfast animals in all the Kingdoms. The greatest artisans in Anacafria embroidered a powerful Goat standing with his front hooves elevated on a giant boulder. The maroon Goat's horns circled backwards and down over muscular shoulders to form the deadly weapons that made the Mountain Goat a formidable and much-feared opponent. Very few men fought a Therian Mountain Goat and came away unscathed. That was true of those who opposed his father as well.

He turned and watched his father as he spoke to his cousin and the commander. Leopold's broad shoulders and powerful arms were a testament to the candlemarks spent in the practice pens wielding his heavy sword and shield. His hands were thick with callouses, the heavy knuckles crisscrossed with jagged white scars from sword fights both practiced and real.

But while Darius admired his father's prodigious fighting skills, it was the ends of his short, blunt fingers—stained with ink from the many candlemarks spent pouring over old records in the royal archives—that impressed the young prince the most. His father was a warrior and a scholar, a man respected by both the nobility and the peasants, by soldiers and by the learned men of the Kingdom.

The prince's gaze moved from his father's hands to his handsome face. Court gossips said that the king's strong, straight nose, high cheekbones and dark wavy hair were proof that somewhere far back in his lineage, one of his ancestors took a Shona princess to his wedding bed.

Darius retrieved the stone he'd been using to sharpen his belt knife. He methodically slid the blade over the rough surface, thinking about his Spirit Guide and the way his life began to change when he and his family rode to Danforth and he'd met his friend, the one the Shona called the Spirit Child.

Bree watched Darius sharpen his dirk and absently listened as Leopold spoke of the possibility of war with their Orgundian neighbors—a kingdom which lay to the northeast across the Cascadian Sea. She wondered how she could protect her Duchy from the Teivaiedin and at the same time help defend the kingdom from an attack by the queen of Organdy. She suddenly realized the king had asked her a question and she'd missed it with her woolgathering. "Pardon, sire?"

The king repeated himself. "I said, I know Baron Ellsworth has been seeing to the running of your duchy, but have you at least been keeping up with your weapons training and tactical skills?"

She shook her head and sighed. "Not as much as I should. When Timur..." Her voice broke and she took a minute to regain her composure. "When she died, I lost all interest in anything but my steading and my wine." She watched the yellow and orange flames dancing in the fire pit before looking back at her king. "Why do you ask? I love you as my king, but I don't want anything to do with political intrigue or with soldiers and war. When we reach the confluence of the rivers, Kaiti and I intend to return to Ashton Fork."

Leopold shook his head, an irritated scowl deepening the lines that stretched the length of his forehead. "Why do I ask? Because I'm going to need all of the experienced commanders I have if it comes to war. Like it or not, right now Bree, you are third in line to the Anacafrian throne. *My* throne. If anything happens to me, you will be one of Darius' main advisors. *Why*, you ask?" He stood and began pacing back and forth in front of the fire.

Bree, Jathez, Darius and Eavan stood as well. The king impatiently waved them back to their seats. "Sit. I need to pace, and you don't need to stand while I do so."

After they'd retaken their seats, the king angrily drew his sword. "As much as I wish it were otherwise," He shook the weapon, "*this* is how we keep Anacafria safe from rulers like Desdamea." He knelt in front of Bree, one knee on the ground, his sword resting casually across the other thigh. "We were pages and squires together for Sir Banyon and Sir Kyels when we'd barely reached our teens. When we became knights, we fought side-by-side during the Estian Wars and the younglings still talk about you as the Hero of the Battle of Blackthorn Pass. Tane's blood, Bree! You saved my life and very nearly lost your own in the process.

"At twenty-eight, you were the sub-commander my mother chose to lead the Huntington's Cavalry in the Queen's Brigade—the most elite cavalry force in all the Kingdoms and the force that helped turn the tide against the Estian Circle!"

"Sire, there are plenty of men and women qualified to lead your troops. I need to return to my steading. That's where I belong now, not on some battlefield trying to—."

Leopold stood and angrily sheathed his sword, the crack of metal against metal loud as he rammed it into place. "I need you, right now, Bree. I trust you, and the soldiers trust you. What I don't need is to have you wallowing away at your steading, drunk and addlebrained!"

He began to pace, running his fingers through his hair in an effort to calm himself. After a deep breath, he returned to sit on the log. He rested his head in his hand, turning his head to face her as he spoke in a softer tone. "I'm sorry Timur is gone. She was my friend with whom I could speak for candlemarks about history and art." A smile lightened his features. "How many times did she say I was dense for discounting the Shona beliefs? No one but Timur would dare say that to her king."

He sat up straight and held Bree's gaze. "I have mourned with you, and I have let you mourn for many months now, Cousin. I will never forget her, but I will not let you foul her memory by sinking into your cups and turning your back on your king and your country."

"Foul her—" Red tinged the corners of her vision as the blood rushed to her head. The ache in her temples multiplied tenfold as her pulse pounded through her veins. She pushed to her feet and glared down at the seated Leopold who quickly rose as well.

Just as she opened her mouth to deliver an angry retort, Ebi, her Badger Spirit Guide, materialized between her and the king. No one but Bree and Kaiti could see or hear her, but that didn't stop the animal from standing on her hind legs and giving Bree a warning shove. *Berate the king in front of these soldiers and they'll turn on you, Duchess. Like it or not, he's right. Not only does he need you, but the child needs you as well.* She poked her paw into Bree's stomach again. *Say the wrong thing now in anger, and the king will have no choice but to turn his back on you both. Is that what you really want?*

Bree looked over at Kaiti, who'd risen to her feet, eyes alert as she watched the drama unfolding.

The guards stood with their heads locked forward, but Bree knew they were using the time-honored technique of any standing man-at-arms; the ability to covertly watch anything of interest through the use of their peripheral vision.

She rubbed her face with the palms of her hands. Ebi was right, and Bree knew it. The troops needed to know that she was loyal to her king and that she trusted his judgment in all areas, particularly in matters of war.

At this point, there was really only one way for her to show unequivocal loyalty to the crown. Shoving down her anger, she took the time to compose herself before turning back and addressing her king. "Your Majesty. I am now and always will be yours to command."

She knelt and drew one of her knives from the bandolier strapped across her chest. Turning the knife so that the tip rested against her heart, she repeated the oath she'd given him on the day of his coronation. "My life for your life, my blood for your blood. I will stand strong and true in defense of your kingdom. My sword will defend you, my words will honor you, and my will shall be obedient to your command. I will defend the defenseless, speak only the truth, and choose loyalty to my king over riches and approbation. This I do swear and will uphold for as long as there is breath in my body."

Relieved, Leopold slowly placed his hand on the hilt of her knife. He spoke clearly, projecting his voice just enough for those listening to hear exactly what he said. "My life for your life, my blood for your blood. I accept your oath of fealty and will protect you and yours throughout the length of my reign. I will be the first into battle and the last to quit the field. I will rule with justice tempered by mercy. This I do swear and will uphold for as long as there is breath in my body."

A roar went up from the ring of soldiers gathered outside the light of the fire.

Startled, Bree saw shadows dancing across scores of smiling faces belonging to the many men and women who heard the commotion and came to see what was happening.

A quick glance also showed her the fierce pride etched onto the faces of the Imperial Guard.

Leopold, his eyes bright with unshed tears, pulled her to her feet and embraced her. He spoke quietly in her ear. "I do need you, Bree. We all need you back, at least until this crisis has run its course."

Bree smiled slightly when Ebi waddled out into the darkness muttering to herself. *Who knew? Maybe she's trainable after all.*

Kaiti came up and gently took the knife out of the king's hand. She looked back and forth between Bree and Leopold, her brows drawn low in confusion and uncertainty. She offered the knife to Bree, who took it and slid it into its sheath without conscious thought.

Turning in a circle, Bree began to recognize many of the faces surrounding them. Each of them lowered their eyes as a sign of respect when she met their gaze. When she came full circle, she found Eavan standing proud and tall next to Nordin, who was his usual stoic self.

Jathez barked at the crowd. "Enough now. Get back to your fires. Eat and rest. We leave before dawn and I'd better not have to come and personally kick your arses out of your tents, or you'll be digging latrines with your spoons for the rest of the trip."

Many of the soldiers chuckled, but they all returned to their tents and cook fires.

Jathez turned to Darius. "That includes you as well, Your Highness. Morning will come early enough, and you always want to make it a habit to be up before your soldiers." He took the prince by the shoulders and bent down to look into his eyes. "Sleep well, young leopard cub."

Obediently, Darius stepped back, bowed to his father and then, out of respect, inclined his head to Jathez and Bree. He tried to stifle the yawn that was threatening to escape, but it appeared just as he turned to go.

His father saw how worn out Darius was and smiled. He wished his son goodnight with the same words he'd been using since the first day the child was born. "I'll be in very soon, Darius. Dream of glory and honor and wake refreshed and ready for a new day."

"I will, Father." Darius sleepily called over his shoulder as he ducked into their pavilion.

Nordin stepped over and took up a position to the right of the entrance.

Eavan began rolling up her mat and putting away the mink oil she'd been using to soften the reins on the king's bridle.

Kaiti helped her as the king turned to Bree and Jathez. "We'll talk more about the possibility of war as we ride through the countryside tomorrow. Whether it actually happens or not, I intend to be better equipped and better prepared than Desdamea and her horde." He placed a hand on Bree's shoulder. "Whether you believe it or not, you're a big part of that, Cousin."

He motioned toward Eavan with his chin and spoke softly. "She's not the only one who idolizes you. Watch the way the soldiers look at you as you ride by. I think you'll be surprised."

Jathez nodded. "Most of the time, heroes don't think they're anything special. In fact, most of them don't even believe they're actually heroes. But our young men and women need leaders they can believe in. People they know have ridden into battle and survived and who can maybe increase their own chances of surviving as well."

He smiled at Bree. "Like it or not, Duchess, that would be you and me." Turning to Leopold, he shrugged, "The king, well, he's the king and his people love him, and his soldiers will follow him without question. I, too, am glad you're back." With that he bowed slightly to the king and retired to his own tent.

Kaiti returned, yawing widely. Bree put her hand over the child's mouth. "Cover your mouth when you do that, especially around nobility."

Leopold chuckled and stepped toward his tent. "Good night you two. Tomorrow will be here earlier than early."

Bree inclined her head toward his retreating back and Kaiti mimicked her movements. The two of them walked to their tent where Kaiti was asleep before her head hit her pillow. Bree knelt and covered her with the blanket. "Goodnight, Little One." She shook her head. "Our lives just took a very strange turn and I hope we're both up for the ride."

CHAPTER 2

The following morning, Bree awoke with a start, disoriented but alert. She'd lived in enough encampments to recognize the sound an army makes as soldiers stoke the fires and fill the cook pots while others strike the tents, pack the mules and saddle the horses. She heard Kaiti outside speaking Shona and was surprised to hear Becca quietly answer. As far as Bree knew, the healer had returned to the tribes to see if she could help with their friend, Taklishim's, recovery. What she was doing here with the king's army was anyone's guess.

When Nashotah, one of the Shona healers, had taken Taklishim back to the camps, no one believed the old shaman would recover from the knife wound he'd received while staying at the sacred cave. But, according to the messengers Becca had sent from the garrison near the Shona encampment, the old man surprised everyone and not only survived, but regained much of his earlier strength.

Just as Bree began rolling up her bedroll, the tent flap pushed aside and Kaiti stuck her head through the opening. "Shimaa! Taklishim." She motioned with her hand for her mother to come outside.

Bree glanced over her shoulder at the child. "Taklishim? Here?" She pointed to the tent wall to make sure the girl understood her meaning.

Kaiti nodded vigorously and once more motioned for Bree to hurry before ducking back out of the tent.

Bree watched as the tent flap fell down into place. "What in Aevala's name is Taklishim doing this far from the Shona lands?"

For the most part, the Shona occupied the Northeastern part of her duchy, their lands encompassing most of the Rittendon Peaks and some of the Ironmoor Forrest. Granted, the king was passing to within a hard day's ride of the Peaks on his way from Orinshire to King's City, but that was still a difficult ride for a man as old as Taklishim.

Becca's voice carried as she greeted one of the soldiers who called out to her from somewhere in the camp. Bree heard the soft gravely voice of her friend, Taklishim, and quickly pulled on her trews. "Well I'll be damned, he is here." She buckled on the sheath that held her short sword balanced between her shoulder blades, pulled on her over-tunic and buckled her bandoliers in place. As she pushed in the last buckle, she called loudly, "Kaiti."

The child pulled the flap up and secured the opening to the side of the tent, letting in some much-needed light as the first rays of dawn began breaking over the horizon.

Bree pointed to their bedrolls and supplies. "You need to pack while I go out to see what's happening." She began to mime rolling up the bags, but Kaiti had already knelt to begin the process of breaking camp.

Most of Kaiti's life had been spent setting up and breaking down camp when she'd lived with the Shona. Bree had never seen anyone quite so quick at the task and marveled at the child's talents. When she finished stowing all of her personal items, Bree stepped outside and saw Becca and Taklishim sitting outside the king's pavilions.

Normally, as the king's squire, Eavan would serve any important guests the king might have. But on this occasion, Bree was gratified to see that Leopold was honoring Taklishim by having the crown prince do the honors.

Eavan brought plates of food for Becca and the king while along-side her Darius made his way carefully toward Taklishim, tongue out as he concentrated on not spilling any of the beans and goat meat he'd piled onto the shaman's plate.

Everyone watched the boy nervously as he hadn't yet begun his training as a page, and as such, wasn't yet skilled in the art of delivering plates of food.

Unlike the worried expressions of the others, Taklishim watched the boy with the quiet dignity the occasion required, his sparkling eyes shining with amusement as Darius made his way toward him. When the prince finally arrived in front of the shaman and handed down the plate to the seated guest, Taklishim schooled his features into a dignified expression. "You honor me, Young Leopard. I could ask for no better service than what you have given me today."

Darius, ever the prince, gave a dignified bow, not as low as he would bow to a king or queen, but very nearly so. "Would you like some drink, Honored Father? Water or wine?"

Bree gave a grunt of approval when the boy addressed the shaman in the same manner a youngling in the tribes would address someone of Taklishim's stature.

Taklishim gave the question serious thought. "I would have some water."

Darius' enthusiasm got the better of him, and he turned and raced to the nearest cooking tent.

The king hid his smile behind his hand and Jathez rolled his eyes.

Bree sat on a nearby log, gratefully accepting a plate from Eavan with a nod. "Thanks, Eavan. I'm starving. Somehow I missed dinner last night." She glanced up plaintively. "Do you think you could find someone who might part with a little Fraval bread at one of the campsites? I know I smelled it last night and for some reason I've developed a craving for it this morning."

The squire's face lit up as she flashed her trademark smile. "Of course. My Auntie's a baker for the Tupper Tane Inn. Do you know the place? Just off the southern road out of town, down a small alleyway and back behind the maklers. She makes the best Fraval bread in the kingdom, and she gave me a few loaves for the trip. I'll be right back!"

After she left to fetch the bread, Darius returned with Taklishim's water, which he handed to the Shaman before stepping behind and to the right of the old man, where he would wait for further instructions.

Jathez, who'd taught many pages and squires during his tenure at the castle, nodded at the boy.

Bree watched as Darius squared his shoulders and stood a little taller before she turned and addressed Taklishim. "I didn't expect you to be here, my friend. Have you completely healed from your wound?" She pointed to her own neck to indicate the slashing he'd taken in the cave.

He ran a finger along the raised welt left by the knife. His voice was even more gravelly than it had been when she'd first met him, most likely due to the injury. "It was Aeval who allowed me to stay. I walked the Paths and spoke with her while I was still in the cave." He paused to swallow painfully, then continued. "She told me I earned the right to pass on to the Second Realm of Tane'iel." He turned shining eyes on Bree. "I spoke to her of my life, of my people, and about the exciting times here on Aevalia I would rather not miss." His eyes darkened. "The return of the Teivaiedin..."

He paused, shaking his head at the thought of the damage the demons had already wrought. "I believe my people, and yours, and even the Spirit Guides need the wisdom and guidance I have gained through my years to once more lock this curse away in Aecheron." He lifted a shoulder. "The goddess allowed me to stay."

As Bree listened to him speak, she wondered how she could possibly have become friends with a man who could walk the pathways and chat with the goddess.

Just then, Eavan returned with a thick slice of bread slathered with golden honey butter.

Bree thanked her for it, then tore the piece in half and offered some to Taklishim.

He took it with a nod of thanks. Before Eavan turned to leave, he stared up into her eyes, partially closing his own as if examining her soul. When finished, he returned to his food without comment.

Eavan politely endured his scrutiny, then glanced at Bree to see if she'd noticed.

She had, but now wasn't the time to question him. Instead, she took a bite of bread, moaning softly as the flavors melted across her tongue. Closing her eyes to fully appreciate the taste without distraction, she let out an involuntary groan of pleasure. "Goddess, Eavan. I've never tasted Fraval bread this good. Do you think I could entice your auntie to come bake for the castle whenever I'm in Orinshire?"

Eavan shrugged. "I'm not sure." She blushed a little. "My Auntie isn't much for nobles. She was that angry when the châtelain chose me to become a page instead of following her into the bakery." She touched the hilt of her short sword. "I was always better with the pokin' than the kneadin'. I could ask her though."

Bree nodded her thanks as she scooped some beans onto her fork. She used the Fraval bread to soak up the juices while listening to Taklishim speaking quietly with the king.

When Jathez saw that Leopold was close to finishing his meal, he gave the orders to pack the last of the dishes, saddle the horses and prepare the wagons.

Bree helped Taklishim stand, then walked with him to a wagon pulled by two Shona warhorses and driven by a young Shona warrior. She made sure he was comfortably wrapped in thick furs before quickly checking the pair of dark bays that made an impressive sight hitched to the front of the cavalry wagon. Jathez must have procured the wagon for the old man to make his travels with the army that much easier on his swollen joints and aching bones.

Kaiti and Bree rode behind his wagon. Bree rode Rebel, and Kaiti proudly sat a gentle mare the queen had given her as a welcoming present several days after Arabetha and the king arrived at Bree's castle at Orinshire. The little mare was white with a smoky-gray mane and tail. Kaiti had named her Miri, after a white streak in the sky the Shona believed was the bushy tail of the White Fox, Miri, who accompanied Aevala on all of her travels through the Realms.

Several candlemarks of quiet riding passed without incident. Just as Bree was wondering when Jathez would call a halt for lunch, Becca trotted up on her roan. She checked to make sure Bree's color was still good after two days of riding. "How're you holding up?"

"Fine. I still get headaches every now and again, but they're getting better." She motioned to the back of the wagon carrying the shaman. "So, I wanted to ask you this morning, why did Taklishim show up at our camp? Is he going to ride with us the entire way to King's City?"

Becca shrugged. "He might. He believes the fate of the Seven Realms is dependent upon the Shona and the Anacafrians working together to defeat the Teivaiedin. He's determined to awaken as many people as he can to the presence of their Spirit Guides. That includes Jathez, Darius, and, most importantly, the king."

Becca's White Wolfe, Garan, spoke as he materialized between the horses. *Fat chance he'll have of awakening the king and his man. The prince, maybe, but Leopold...* Rebel and the roan ignored him, but Kaiti's Miri pricked her ears forward and began prancing sideways.

Bree grabbed the mare's reins near the bridle and pulled her in close to Rebel's side. "Must you always drop in unexpectedly like that? You just spooked Kaiti's horse."

Garan trotted forward until he could get a good look at Miri under Rebel's neck. *Spooked? She has the heart of a warrior. She's simply excited to see such a magnificent specimen from another Realm.*

Bree looked to her right and left, then over her shoulder. "And just where would that specimen be hiding?"

Garan barked a laugh. *A cruel, cruel arrow to my heart.*

The big wolf's shoulders came to about the middle of Becca's calf when she was in her saddle. She reached down and scratched between his shoulder blades. "Has anyone had any luck finding Rhia'en?"

Bree looked at Becca. "Who's Rhia'en?"

She's the Guide for Zia, Taklishim's daughter. She went missing two days ago, and no, Sheyah, no one has found her yet. Denabi and I have been concentrating on searching Bendi since that's Rhia'en's home Realm.

Bree knew that some of the Spirit Guides had recently been killed walking the pathways, and she wondered if that was Rhia'en's fate. "What kind of Guide is she?"

"A civet. Not very aggressive or assertive. I think that's why Zia's husband, Tsoe can bully her so easily."

"Do you think she's dead like those other Guides who were staked out along the pathways?"

You say 'staked out' as though it were a small thing, Duchess. Garan's throaty growl brought Bree up short. *To stake out and blood one of the Peshár is to remove us from existence forever.* The White Wolf, who was still trotting between Rebel and the roan, looked over his shoulder at Bree.

She is still alive. As we all discovered when the Teivaiedin first appeared, if a Guide is killed by them, the apprentice dies as well. Zia lives, so we know Rhia'en lives. The time where Spirit Guides were immortal has passed. Even the gods search their dimensions for her. Bendith, of the Third Realm, especially so since she is of his Realm in this lifetime.

They rode on in silence, each one wrestling with their own thoughts about the Teivaiedin. The landscape they rode through was becoming more and more open with meadows of yellow grass stretching out on either side of the trail. Off in the distance, Bree could barely see the evergreen trees that filled the Forest of Aeval. That meant they were nearing the border of Danforth and would soon leave her duchy and enter Cafria.

Garan lifted his nose high. *Ugh, the dust down here is ruining my glossy shine.* With that, he loped forward and jumped into the wagon where Taklishim lay resting.

Becca watched him go. "Rhia'en is such a gentle Guide. I wish I could walk the paths and help search for her."

"I've been thinking, Becs. We're going to be fighting the war on both fronts—the Teivaiedin and possibly Organdy. The king made it clear to me that my first allegiance is to him if war breaks out, but, if every person has a Spirit Guide, and the Teivaiedin win and are able to stake out and blood all of the Spirit Guides, doesn't that mean every one in Anacafria will be dead as well?" Bree hoped she was wrong, but the piercing look Becca gave her told her that her thinking was right on the mark.

Becca ran her hand through the roan's black mane. "Why do you think Aevala allowed Taklishim to stay? By all rights, he was a dead man in the cave. He'd lost more blood than even a healthy young warrior can lose and still survive, let alone an old man with one foot hovering over his grave. In all the Shona legends, I've never heard of that happening. And why do you think Taklishim is here, riding in the back of a wagon on his way to King's City?"

Bree looked to the head of the column where the king rode his chestnut stallion. "I know Kaiti is important to the Spirit Guides, and to the battle with the Teivaiedin, but she's coming with me to King City, and then probably on campaign. I have Ellsworth to see to the

Duchy while I'm with the king, but if she's with me, how can she help the Guides in the battles for the spiritual realm?"

Kaiti heard her name and glanced over at her mothers. They seemed to be in a serious conversation about something, but she still didn't understand all of their words. She did recognize the tension in the air, however, and that worried her. Twice now, her first mother sent her away, and even though she'd told her that would never happen again, Kaiti didn't fully trust her word. Leaning forward so she could see around Bree to Becca, she asked the healer, "Is she talking about sending me away?"

Becca, who spoke both Shona and Anacafrian, answered immediately. "No. We're talking about the battles that are coming." She pointed to the front, and then swung her arm around, indicating the entire army surrounding them. "The king is gathering his soldiers to fight with his neighbor who comes from across the great sea, and we also have the Teivaiedin to battle. She's wondering how she can help with both enemies at the same time."

To Kaiti's way of thinking, fighting battles on two fronts was much better than being sent away again. "That's good. Fighting battles is bad but being sent away is worse."

"Kaiti, Bree gave you her word she'd never send you away again. You have to believe her. You're going to have to learn her language, though, because I won't always be around to translate."

Bree listened to the two of them and wondered what they were talking about.

Becca saw the frustration on her friend's face and told her what Kaiti had said.

Bree looked down at the girl, then back at Becca. "I really did some damage by sending her away, but I'm torn between taking her on campaign if a war breaks out and sending her back to the tribes with you. Queen Arabetha also gave me the option of having her stay with her at the castle, but I don't think that would work." She sighed. "But luckily I don't need to come to a decision right this second. Today I'm enjoying the ride on this ornery old boy." She patted Rebel's neck, which reminded her of something she'd meant to follow up on with her friend. "When you went back to Ashton

Fork, were you able to find anyone who could take care of my animals for me?"

"I did, and I think you'll like my solution. Do you remember Alilya and Bennet Coles? They're the ones we met on the trail who were moving to Ashton Fork. Remember? They were riding in the coach with their daughter who was Kaiti's age."

"I remember. I told them to find Mauran when they got there."

"Well, do you also remember that small piece of land Emi and Mardi Stiles

cleared behind the Temple of Aeval?"

Bree glanced thoughtfully at her friend. "Didn't they die the same time as Timur?" Bree's wife, Timur, died when a particularly virulent form of influenza raced through the villages of Ashton Fork and Foxtail Run, killing nearly a third of the inhabitants of both places.

Nodding, Becca continued, "The land's been lying vacant, and Mauran asked for a village vote about whether to give the property to Bennet and Alilya. The vote was unanimous, except for old Jerin, who wouldn't vote aye even if it were his own mother who needed the help. Anyway, they didn't have anywhere to stay while they built their cabin, so I made them a deal. I told them they could live in your steading if they would take care of the animals and your plantings." She glanced at Bree out of the corner of her eye. "And I asked them to tend Timur's gardens as well." That last made her slightly nervous since Bree hadn't allowed anyone to help her bury her wife or help tend her burial garden.

Bree thought about that a minute. She didn't like the idea of people living in her home, and she especially didn't want them in Timur's garden, but she couldn't ask the neighbor to keep going twice a day to feed her animals either. "They seemed like good enough people. Do either Bennet or Alilya know anything about animals? I'm not sure, but I think they might have been part of the nobility of Organd—" The thought hit her like a lightning bolt. She turned and stared at Becca.

The healer caught her friend's sudden alert expression. "What?"

"Becs, they're from Organdy, remember? That tells me they're either spies sent to blend into Anacafrian society, or they're a wealth of important information on what is really happening in Desdamea's kingdom. Either way, when you go back, you're going to have to figure out which it is."

"I'm pretty sure it's the latter. I spoke with them when I helped them move into your steading. Alilya is actually third cousin to the queen. Do you remember the attempted coup last summer? You know, when half of Desdamea's nobles rose up against her?"

Bree nodded.

"Well, Alilya's father was one of the leaders. Desdamea beheaded both him and his wife. Alilya, Bennet and Cylia Mari were barely able to flee. They were lucky. Bennet was a trader who did most of his business with the trading ships that sailed into Port Aret. A captain friend of his smuggled the three of them onto his ship and snuck out of the harbor in the middle of the night."

"That makes sense. I remember Alilya not wanting anyone to know she was from Organdy. If that's the case, I'll speak to Jathez about sending one of his spies to go talk to them. Their inside knowledge might just prove invaluable."

As though he'd heard his name, Jathez glanced over his shoulder at them before calling a halt for the midday meal.

Bree and Kaiti rode to the front of the column to join Leopold and Darius while Becca went to Taklishim's wagon to make sure he was faring well on the journey. They were typically given a candlemark for the midday meal, and everyone was happy even for that short amount of time out of the saddle.

CHAPTER 3

Bree blocked Kalsik's downward blow with the wooden blade of her practice sword. Jathez had halted the column after seven candlemarks of travel, and after dinner Bree decided there was no time like the present to begin the long process of beating her body back into fighting shape.

Kalsik served on Darius' protection detail precisely because of his skill with the sword. He also trained common soldiers, squires, and knights alike during his tenure at King's City.

Early in his reign, Leopold had decreed that everyone who fought under his banner must have access to skilled instruction. To that end, he provided trainers for every man and woman under his command, regardless of rank or age.

Kalsik pivoted left, bringing his sword low across his body, telegraphing an obvious strike to Bree's midsection.

The second Bree moved to counter, she knew she'd been had.

Kalsik waited for her weight to shift as she blocked his feint, and when it did, he caught the edge of her blade on his and forced both swords up high. He grabbed her sword arm in his free hand before angling the tip of his own sword downward, stopping inches from Bree's exposed neck.

Bree shook her head and pushed the sword aside before bracing her hands on her knees to catch her breath. "That's the sixth time you've killed me. I used to be able to drag you pups all over the practice pens before taking you out. Now look at me." She held the leather of her trews between fingers and palms and watched the sweat drip from her brow and land in the dirt at her feet.

Kalsik retrieved a towel from Kaiti who watched from the sidelines. He winked at the child before handing the towel to Bree. "Your technique is better than most, Your Grace. Your problem is that you've lost muscle, both here," He touched her upper arm, "and here—" he pointed to her midsection, "— that you need to wield the sword. If you really intend to get back into fighting shape, every night and every morning you should ask Rocca if you could borrow his sword to practice your forms. He's a big man, and his weapon is heavier than most. Once you bring your muscles back to fighting form, I'll lay odds you'll beat me more often than you lose."

Bree accepted the proffered towel. She looked up at the handsome young man with the aristocratic face and curly brown hair. His lean, muscular body towered over her so that that even she needed to raise her chin to look into his eyes. His gambeson and his boots were made of good quality leather, as was his halberd, although the shine was worn off from years of battle and practice. She tried to guess his age and finally asked, "Were you old enough to fight in the Estian wars?"

He raised his eyebrows. "Yes, just barely. If you can call being a squire to Sir Jensin of Deerford Duchy being in a war. He was already an old knight then and didn't see much battle. But it was all very exciting for a young lad of thirteen summers. I think that's part of why King Leopold assigned me to Prince Darius. I know what it's like to be in a war at such a young age."

"Your family's from Deerford then?"

He shot her a mischievous grin. "You don't recognize me, do you, Your Grace?"

Bree studied his face. Nothing about the young man was familiar, until she actually focused on the distinct, greenish gray eyes that held tiny flecks of gold throughout. "Don't tell me you're one of Gregrin's brood? He's sired so many children I'm sorry to say I lost track. I seem to remember he named one of his sons Kalsik, but that's such a common name I never made the connection."

Even though Gregrin was her uncle, she'd never been especially close to his family. His first wife, Vichois, was a mean-spirited harridan who'd spitefully done everything she could to demean Bree and her skills as a warrior. Jealousy, and a slight trace of insanity, ran strongly in her blood. In Bree's mind, it had been no great loss when Vichois had left Gregrin for a wealthier and much younger noble from the northern Duchy of Salth.

Kalsik gave her a playful bow, swinging his arm across his midsection in a dramatic gesture. "Kalsik Redland Leopold Amranth, Viscount Zarad, of the Duchy of Deerford, at your service, Madame."

Bree laughed at his self-deprecating manner. She liked the young man and could clearly see why Leopold wanted Darius to spend time with him. "Where did you learn your excellent swordsmanship?" She pointed at the five concentric circles embroidered on his left sleeve. "Jathez appointed you a senior instructor at a fairly young age. That takes some doing."

He took her practice sword and held both his and hers in one big hand while he spoke. "I'm the eighth son of a duke, tenth bairn out of thirteen living offspring. I knew I'd never inherit Deerford." He shrugged. "And most of the good steadings in the duchy have already been claimed by my older brothers and sisters, so I decided to make a name for myself as a knight. I think you knew our arms master at Deerford, Sir Negril Richond?"

A smile lit Bree's face. "Of course. One of the best swordsmen I've ever known. If he tutored you in the art, it's no wonder you've become so proficient." Bree glanced over her shoulder as Eavan ran up.

"Your Grace. The king needs to see you. He says it's urgent."

Bree nodded her thanks to Kalsik and handed him her towel before starting for the king's pavilion. She hesitated a moment, then turned back to the young man who was inspecting the wooden edges of both swords for damage. "Kalsik, I've seen you training Darius in weapons practice. Would you consider training Kaiti as well?"

Kalsik hesitated, and Bree wondered if it was because Kaiti was considered a Shona half-breed. She sighed with relief when he walked over and took Kaiti's forearm in his big hand and measured it with a thumb and forefinger.

"She's too small for the regular practice swords. With your permission, I'll take her to the weapon's smith and ask him to fashion her one that would fit her hand as well as her reach." He turned the little girl in a circle. "I doubt she'll ever grow tall enough to battle anyone conventionally, but I'll teach her some tricks I taught my younger sister, Yoren, when she wanted to become a knight."

"Your Grace..." Eavan anxiously gestured for Bree to attend the king.

"Right. That would be excellent, thank you, Kalsik. You can take her after supper tonight, if you will." She turned and once again began following Eavan. When the young woman began wending her way through the encampment instead of going straight to the king's tent, Bree wondered where they were headed. "The king's not at his pavilion?"

Eavan shook her head. "No. Taklishim had that young warrior of his set up their tent on the outskirts of the encampment. The king was over talking to him when a messenger arrived from Port Suliet."

Several of the soldiers politely greeted Bree as she strode through the camp and she absently nodded at each one as she passed. She kept a standing militia at Orinshire and had brought about two hundred soldiers along at the king's request. More would follow once Ellsworth gathered them from the outlying areas. Since the king wanted her back as one of his lord commanders, she needed able-bodied men and women to augment the soldiers already sworn to her standard. But she needed more than just the fighting force, she'd also need the camp regulars; the cooks, tanners, hunters, and blacksmiths so critical to the running of an army on the move.

Bree acknowledged a woman she recognized as one of the Orinshire cooks with a nod and a smile. The portly woman lowered her chin in a curt nod before turning to a young boy and chastising him for watching the duchess instead of stirring the stew. "Gi' ya' peepers on ta' stew, ya' scal'wag! Ah'll nowt be servi' burnt choppins' cuz a' da likes o' you!"

The scamp threw Bree an oversized smile full of dazzling, white teeth and twinkling eyes before pulling off his cap and dropping into deep bow. He then dodged a swipe by the cook as he quickly grabbed the spoon and began stirring the black iron cook pot vigorously.

His jaunty smile told Bree everything she needed to know about the woman. She was a fair but strict taskmaster who knew how to run a rough trail kitchen full of soldiers and hardened camp followers.

Bree almost reached the perimeter of the camp when a man's over-loud, gruff snarl filled the evening air.

"Get tha' friggi' Dado out a' da' camp! She don' belong wit' ta' decent likes ah' us!"

Bree, recognizing the term, dado, as the derogatory, lower class slang for a halfbreed, immediately swung toward the voice, trying to identify the one who'd spoken. She didn't need to look very far or very long.

Out of the corner of her eye she saw Rocca barreling down on an ill-kempt soldier standing next to one of the two-man tents. But what was more interesting, to Bree at least, was the cook she'd just passed holding up her skirts and running toward the man wielding a large metal ladle high above her head.

When the foul-mouthed soldier realized both Rocca and the cook were coming for him, he dropped the plate he'd been eating from and ran.

A foot soldier in Bree's livery shoved the man as he ran past, sending him flying head first into the dirt.

The cook reached him and began whacking him mercilessly with the heavy cup end of the ladle as soldiers whooped and cheered her on.

The surprised look on Rocca's face as he pulled up short would have been comical if the situation hadn't been so distasteful.

A commanding voice rose above the din. "Here! What's this? Off him, Woman! Let him up!" Jathez strode over and bodily lifted the red-faced, angry-eyed cook away from her hapless victim. He set her on her feet and barked, "Now what's this all about?"

Several angry faces glared down at the man's bloody, swollen face.

He was an ugly brute even before the beating, with his thick lips and forehead, and fuzzy eyebrows that fell down over the top of his eyes. His trews were filthy even before the cook pummeled him into the dirt and his red under-kirtle showed through several unpatched holes in his tunic.

He nervously flicked his tongue through a gap created by two missing front teeth.

When no one answered, Jathez pointed to Rocca. "You. I want to know exactly what happened. You know perfectly well I don't tolerate this kind of brawling in my camps and I saw you running to join in."

Rocca snapped to attention. "Dis flee bitten excuse for eur saldia called t' young'un eur Dado. It's not reet 'n ah won't stan' for it!" At the last second, he remembered he was addressing the Lord Commander of the Imperial Guards. "Sir!"

Jathez turned his glare on the man cowering at his feet. His lip curled in disgust as he swung back to Rocca, who pulled himself even straighter than he'd been a few seconds earlier. "Get all of his things and escort him from camp. We don't need vermin like him in the king's armies."

Striding angrily over to Kaiti, Jathez turned her so she faced away from him. He hoisted her high into the air. The child could have been a small ragdoll for all the effort it took to raise her high above his head.

Unsure what was happening, Kaiti grabbed onto his muscular forearms and held on.

"I want this known by everyone in this camp and by the entirety of Leopold's army. This child is Kaiti Makena, the adopted daughter of the Duchess, Aurelia Makena. That makes her cousin to King Leopold and Queen Arabetha. As such she is under my personal protection. Anyone," He lowered Kaiti to the ground and met the stares of as many people as possible, "And I mean *anyone*, who insults her, insults me. If you harm her, you harm me. Are there any questions?"

Everyone stood motionless, not wanting to draw attention to themselves.

The bleeding soldier pushed to his feet. Spittle flew from the hole between his teeth as he angrily spat out his defense. "'Ow c'n ye' be difindin' the dado, yer lordship? Sh's a filthy pi' a' vermin a' don' b'long near ta' king's armies. I be loyal ta' da' king, I be! Sh's a dado!"

Ignoring the man's outburst, Jathez turned and bellowed for his squire. "Cameron!"

"Here, sir." A thin, scholarly looking fellow with curly brown hair trailing down to his shoulders stepped around Rocca where he'd been completely hidden by the huge bulk of the Ironmoor native. The young man wore a perfectly fitted silk tunic, clean trews made of fine wool, and a black velvet cap with intricately colored embroidery sewn into the cuff.

Jathez gave a dismissive flick of his hand toward the unkempt soldier. "Go with Rocca. I want this vermin's name recorded in the Book of Opprobrium. He'll not be allowed to hold any positions in the king's armies. Make sure—"

The man gave a strangled howl as he made a grab for Kaiti, who was quite adept at leaping away from grasping hands. She dodged behind Bree and he came face-to-face with the murderous glare of an infuriated duchess protecting her young.

Surprisingly, Rocca was just as quick as Kaiti and had his big, ham-sized fist clasped around the man's scrawny neck before anyone else could react. He lifted him off his feet and hauled him around until they were both facing Jathez. Rocca once again came to attention, this time holding his squirming, foul-mouthed trophy two inches off the ground. The muscles in Rocca's forearm flexed slightly and the man gave a tiny squawk and quit struggling.

Jathez continued as if nothing out of the ordinary had happened. "—you strip him of any clothing, tools, or equipment he received as part of his contract." He glanced around him. "Does anyone know what his position was?"

The cook spoke up. "I'd nowt be claimin' 'im 'cept 'e uz 'signed ta' da cookin' wagin'. Gaed riddance ta' da' spew up." With that pronouncement she spat on the man's shirt, grabbed her ladle from where she'd dropped it in the dirt and strode briskly back to the cook fire. She cuffed her helper on the ear for once more forgetting to stir the pot.

Bree watched her go, then shifted her attention to Rocca, who was hauling his trophy to one of the tents.

Cameron turned to follow, but Bree called him over to where she stood with Kaiti. "Cameron, a word please."

He turned and immediately doffed his cap, holding his front leg straight out with a pointed toe and bowing deeply to her in a perfect courtier's flection. "Yes, Your Grace?"

Bree glanced over the boy's head at Jathez, who shrugged and rolled his eyes.

When Cameron rose from his bow, he held his cap on his chest with both hands, waiting patiently.

Bree nodded in the direction of the cook. "She's from Orinshire."

Curious as to what Bree wanted with his squire, Jathez narrowed his eyes but remained silent.

She turned to the lord commander and asked, "I assume I'll be allowed to pick my own officers and staff?"

Jathez nodded. "Within certain parameters, yes. There are some men and women that I, and some of my sub-commanders, would prefer to keep."

"Then Cameron, if she isn't already spoken for, I'd like her to be the first person assigned to my battalion. She'll be in charge of the other cooks and all of the staff needed to feed my men and women. Please get with her about who she'd like to see working for her in those positions."

Cameron gaped.

To Bree's experienced eye, he'd obviously never held a field position. In fact, she wondered if this was his first time outside the confines of the castle.

"But, but, Your Grace...you can have the best of any of the king's staff..." He shot a confused, pleading look at Jathez. "Sir, it would be a disgrace for someone like—" He pointed at the cook. "— that woman to serve as head of...of...the duchess' entire commissary."

Bree put her hand on his shoulder. "Cameron. I'm going to give you the benefit of the doubt, because I know Jathez wouldn't have you as his squire if you weren't intelligent and capable of handling all the minutia he deals with on a daily basis."

Cameron's face lit up with her praise.

"However, you have to have an open mind if you're going to serve him in the field. People like that woman," She pointed at the cook, "are more valuable to a standing army than even the most experienced knights. Open your mind and curb your prejudice if you want to serve Jathez well."

Cameron blushed. "Commander Jathez has told me the exact same thing." He met Bree's gaze. "I'll try, Your Grace. Forgive me."

Bree removed her hand. "Keep an open mind and there'll be nothing to forgive."

"Bree! For God's sakes, Woman! How long do plan to keep your liege waiting when he sends his squire to summon you? Did Eavan mention that it was urgent?" The king came striding through the encampment, oblivious to the men and women who jumped to their feet and bowed as he strode past. "Damn it, Jathez, you too? Doesn't it mean anything to anyone around here that the king has called for a meeting of *both* the lord commanders and *all* of the marshals?"

The amused glint in Bree's eyes didn't escape the king's notice. She dipped her head and said, "I'm sorry, Your Majesty. We had some issues come up that needed to be dealt with sooner rather than later." She swept her hand forward. "If you'll lead the way, Sire, we're ready to join you immediately."

Leopold's eyes narrowed as he glared first at Bree, and then at Jathez. He was normally cool and collected, and Bree wondered what happened to put him this much on edge. He pivoted on his heel and strode briskly back the way he'd come.

Bree, Jathez, and Eavan fell into step behind him, with Kaiti bringing up the rear. Once again, people bowed as the king walked past.

He spoke over his shoulder to the lord commander. "Jathez, I realize it's been a while since I've been in the field with my troops, but please pass the word that I don't expect them to bow every time I come near or walk close to their tents."

Jathez nodded. "Yes, M'lord. I'll have the heralds spread the word."

"Good." Leopold ducked into the council tent that had been erected next to the smaller one in which Taklishim was staying.

Bree paused to look at the Shona tent because she'd never seen one constructed in quite the same way before. Animal skins made up the thick, stiff, round base. They'd been dried in such a way as to make them malleable enough to fold for travel, yet stiff enough to stand on their own when pulled into a circular shape and staked at intervals around the circumference. A second canvas of animal skins stretched across the top, fully covering the structure.

"Bree!"

"Coming, Sire." She joined Jathez and Eavan who'd followed the king into the tent opening.

Kaiti ducked inside and made herself as invisible as possible by squatting near the opening to wait.

Several of the higher-ranking marshals stood around a table set in the center of the common area. The marshals ranked directly under Jathez and Bree, and each normally commanded five regiments of one hundred soldiers each, although their numbers could swell much higher during a full-scale war. As more and more legions answered the king's mandated call for troops from the outer lying duchies, baronies, and fiefs, the king would appoint more marshals from within the ranks of the nobility. Being named a marshal was a high honor generally bestowed upon noble firstborn sons who either distinguished themselves in battle or who excelled in their tactical knowledge and expertise.

Taklishim sat to the side on a leather tripod stool, with the warrior who'd accompanied him standing patiently by his side.

Prince Darius waited next to Becca, whom Bree assumed was there as a translator.

In the far corner of the tent, an exhausted herald waited for them to assemble. Judging by the gold and maroon stripes around his sleeve, he was a member of the Royal Messenger Service, an elite group of men and women who stopped at nothing, short of death, to deliver their messages for the king.

The herald swayed slightly, then unobtrusively caught himself by resting a hand on a small, wooden side-table. His fingers trembled, and by the look of him, Bree guessed his weakness stemmed from sheer and utter exhaustion. A thin layer of red silt covered his skin and clothing and a combination of sweat and muddied clay streaked his blunt-nosed face. His brown, curly hair lay plastered to his head and hung in wet, dirty ringlets down past his shoulders.

The king impatiently motioned to his squire, "Eavan, get this man a stool and something to eat and drink. I'd rather he gives his report sitting than flat on his back after he falls exhausted at our feet."

Several of the marshals looked up, and one whom Bree didn't recognize hurried over to get a stool. "Tane's blood, man, speak up. I should have seen how exhausted you were when you first arrived. Here, have a seat before you drop."

A second marshal—this one Bree recognized as Lord Jeffries, the Earl of Guildenhall—sneered at his counterpart before turning back to the map stretched across the table. "Oh, do relax, Sandresin. It's only a messenger doing his job. There's no need to coddle the man."

Sandresin placed the stool near the side-table anyway. Bree took note of his name so she could remember to ask Jathez to assign Marshal Sandresin to her battalion.

After the messenger sat and accepted a cup of mead from Eavan, the king stepped to the table. "Now that everyone's here, Marok, let's hear your report one more time, and then my squire will provide you with a warm tent and plenty of food and drink to help you get back on your feet."

The man began to rise, but Leopold gently pushed him back onto the stool "You're about dead, man. We'll dispense with the formalities this time."

Looking extremely uncomfortable sitting in such an august assembly when everyone else, except Taklishim, was standing, the man took a deep breath and began to speak. His voice was a strong baritone typical of most men chosen for messenger duty. "Two days ago, the governor of Port Suliet sent a dispatch to Duke Westin of Salth."

Not able to stand his discomfort any longer, he stood and addressed the king. "Please, Your Majesty, I'll be more comfortable standing." When Leopold nodded, the man tugged on the bottom of his tunic in a futile attempt to pull out the wrinkles, brought himself to attention and began from the beginning.

"Two days ago, the governor of Port Suliet sent a dispatch to Duke Westin of Salth. A captain of a trading vessel arrived in port claiming he'd just come from Port Connel in Organdy. He said Queen Desdamea has assembled twenty sailing vessels in the bay, each capable of transporting two hundred soldiers. The captain said that at night, even on those nights lacking a moon, he'd look landward and the entire hillside as far as the eye could see was so bright with cook fires a blind man would have sworn it was daylight."

Unease spread through the tent. The four marshals murmured among themselves and Leopold held up his hand for silence.

The messenger continued, "The captain almost didn't make it out of Port Connel. The only reason he was allowed to sail was because he held a previously approved manifest granting him passage to the Blue Aisles. He said once he'd cleared the Seven Circles, he turned west instead of east and came to warn the king."

Leopold took the man's empty cup off the side-table and handed it to Eavan to refill. "Do you know the captain's name?"

"Yes, Your Majesty. Captain Le'roy of the trading ship, Pelican."

Turning to Jathez, the king pointed to some parchment on the table. "Make sure to send Captain Le'roy a reward for risking his ship to come warn us about the possible invasion. Make it substantial enough that others know I reward loyalty well."

Jathez looked to Cameron, who'd entered the tent while the king was speaking. He briskly dipped his chin in the young man's direction and his squire acknowledged the silent order with a slight bow.

Maps covered most of the table, and Bree walked over to see what the marshals were studying so intently. "How will you corroborate the information? From what I understand, most of our spies within Organdy have been returned without their heads."

Very quietly, Taklishim spoke to Leopold from the corner of the room. "Your father, King Pries, scattered my people to the four winds. Some even chose to flee far across the waters, into the land you know as Organdy. Tonal, the Spirit Guide of their Chief, met me on the pathways and told of a great army assembling on their shores."

Marshal Jeffries scoffed, "A Spirit Guide? You expect us to declare war on a country based on a creature from mythology?" He waived his hand through the air, palm down, completely dismissing the old man. "You need to hold your tongue, Old Man. We listen to facts. We don't need to play your Shona make-believe games." The sharp angles of his cheekbones emphasized the hatred burning behind his eyes.

The warrior standing behind Taklishim reached for the knife he carried in an ornately decorated sheath.

Becca, who'd taught the young man to speak and understand the Anacafrian language, stepped forward and put her hand on his arm. She spoke quietly in the Shona tongue. "Peace, Tisneé. He's an arrogant fool. The king will address his rudeness."

Reluctantly, Tisneé released his grip on the knife and once again stood guard behind his chief.

Just as Becca predicted, Leopold stepped close to Jeffries, his eyes narrowed in barely suppressed anger. He spoke in a chillingly calm voice. "I know the Shona killed your father when he tried to move them off your family's lands, Jeffries, but this man is my honored guest. I expect you to treat him as such. Do I make myself clear?"

Jeffries' lips pulled into a tight, thin line. He nodded curtly, then turned as if to study the map again.

Leopold addressed Taklishim. "Thank you for that information. We need to gather knowledge from every available source if we're to defeat Desdamea."

Taklishim was not only a shaman. He was known throughout Anacafria as one of the fiercest, most tactically dangerous chiefs to ever lead warriors into battle. A breeze wafted through the slight opening where the tent flap hadn't completely dropped back into place. Taklishim glanced at the opening, then gathered his ceremonial blanket tighter around his chest before once again addressing the king. "This enemy threatens my people as well as yours. There will come a time when your soldiers must fight alongside my warriors. You must prepare them for such a time."

Red-faced, Jeffries growled as he once again turned to face Taklishim. The king held up his hand to stop him.

Marshal Sandresin's lip curled in disgust as he stared at Jeffries' back. He shouldered his way past the arrogant man to address Taklishim. "I'd be honored to have any of your warriors fight alongside me and my soldiers. I've seen your people fight, Taklishim."

Jeffries shoved the younger man out of his way. "Don't be a fool, Sandresin! The Shona can't be trusted. They rape and kill our women, they—" Jeffries glanced around until he found Kaiti sitting quietly near the opening to the tent.

He strode over to her and practically wrenched her arm from its socket to show everyone the tattoo on her forearm. "How do you think she came to live with the Shona? A girl from the Otsmeadow Alliance? They butchered her family! That's how!"

Bree reacted the instant he'd twisted Kaiti's arm. She lunged for the man, grabbing the front of his gambeson and twisting the collar tight around his neck.

Jathez wrapped his arms around her chest and pulled her off him.

The two other marshals, who'd remained silent up to that point, grabbed Jeffries and dragged him behind the table.

Bree angrily threw off Jathez' arms and jabbed a finger in Jeffries' face. "Touch her again, Jeffries, and your family will have to search for the pieces of your body I leave scattered around the dung heap for the buzzards."

Becca stepped up next to Bree. She didn't dare touch a man of Jeffries' rank, but she could stand beside her friend in a show of solidarity.

Every tendon in Jeffries' neck stretched taut as he screamed at Bree from across the table. "*You* have disgraced this kingdom and every noble in it by bringing that filthy child and that unholy barbarian into the presence of the king! If King Leopold doesn't see it, he's no less a fool than Sandresin!" Spittle flew from his mouth as he continued his tirade. "And you dare lay hands on me?" He struggled with the men holding his arms. "*You dare?*"

Everyone except Bree looked to the king, who stood rigid while waiting for the tirade to end. When he'd heard enough, he stalked to where the men held Jeffries, took hold of the pendant that granted him the lands and titles of the Earl of Guildenhall and ripped it from his neck. "Your *fool* of a king says this, Merand Jeffries. You have disobeyed my command and disgraced yourself in my presence. As I bestowed them upon you, so now I strip you of your titles and your lands. Your family is forfeit to my kingdom and must be gone from my lands within the fortnight. According to custom, if any of your progeny or household wishes to petition me for the right to stay, let them come before me and beg my mercy."

Leopold turned to Jathez. "Get him out of my sight."

Jathez motioned to the two marshals who half carried, half walked a white-faced Jeffries from the tent.

No one spoke while the king stared down at the pendant he held in his hand.

Unsure what had just happened, a frightened Kaiti stepped over to Tisneé, who put his arm across her shoulders. Her heart pounded painfully, and the instinct to run clashed with her need to stay.

Denabi materialized and brushed against her leg. *Stand tall and strong, Little Kitten. Do you see how Taklishim is unshaken by the man's words? You must learn to let the hatred of petty men slide off you in just the same way*

Taklishim lifted his too thin arm and gently brushed his gnarled hand through the fur on the Cat's wide shoulders.

When Jathez and the marshals returned, the king dropped the pendant onto the table. "Who else questions my decision to allow the child to stay with the duchess?" When no one answered, he turned to Taklishim. "We all know that some of your people killed her family when they stole her away. In that at least Jeffries was correct. The raids by the renegade Shona must stop if we have any hope of creating an alliance between our people."

Taklishim stayed quiet a moment before finally answering. "And the butchering of my people by yours? There is a reason my children's hatred runs deeper than the Tegonque River. We used to be numbered as the great elk, thousands living peacefully together as one nation. Now, we are few. The killing on both sides must stop. I will give my word, and my word will go out among my people, and my word is law. What will you do, King Leopold?"

Leopold thought for a long moment. Finally, he pulled off the signet ring he wore on his right index finger. "I will once again send out messengers to every corner of my kingdom, proclaiming an end to hostilities with the Shona." He looked down at the ring, then back into Taklishim's eyes. "I will give my word, and my word will go out among my people, and my word is law."

He turned to Jathez, who understood the implicit command in the king's quick nod. "I'll have Cameron draw up the proclamation, Sire. We'll word it slightly stronger than the last missive you sent out. Unfortunately, as we have just seen, there are still holdouts among some of the land holders who've had to battle to keep their lands out of Shona hands."

Becca noticed the muscles of Tisneé's jaws ripple and knew the young warrior's thoughts. Anacafrians and Shona had lived peacefully for hundreds, perhaps thousands of years until King Pries decided he wanted the lands the Shona claimed for their own. Tisneé had been raised to one day become a chief among his people. Taklishim had done an admirable job of teaching the young man the art of diplomacy. If he decided to speak, she was interested to know how he would approach the issue.

The young warrior stepped forward to address the king. "The battle is difficult because the lands you speak of are not the lands of your people, but rather the lands of mine. Your father gave away land that was not his, to people who should not be living there. This is the reason your holders must battle to keep the lands out of Shona hands. If you want peace, and if you want the strength of our warriors to assist you in your battles, perhaps you should recall your holders back to land that is truly theirs."

Taklishim raised a gnarled hand and placed it on Tisneé's forearm. "My warrior speaks from deep within the Shona soul. Listen to the truth of his words." He indicated the tent opening with his free hand. "The man you banished, and his father, destroyed an entire village, raped the women and staked out the men for the vultures to eat while they yet lived."

The shocked expression on Leopold's face spoke volumes. "That can't be true. I would never tolerate such behavior from one of my nobles." He looked to Jathez for confirmation.

The lord commander seemed just as nonplused as the king. "I know that during your father's reign such atrocities were commonplace, but I've never heard of anyone daring to act in such a way during your rule, Your Majesty. When Lord Jeffries—by that I mean Merand Jeffries' father—was killed, we were told it was while protecting his family from a Shona attack."

Tisneé raised his chin. He stared out of eyes that bore an uncanny resemblance to those of his Spirit Guide, the Shengali Hawk, Azeel. "What you say is true. The Shona warriors attacked in retribution for the killing that took place in the village. My father's sister's son was staked out and left to die." His voice broke on his next words. "He had only twelve winter moons."

No one spoke until a horrified Sandresin broke the silence. "They staked out a twelve-year-old boy and left him to die?"

The king pointed to the maps laid out on the table. "Tisneé, do you know how to read maps?"

The young man joined the king, studying the parchment a moment before shaking his head. "I don't read your words, and the lands do not seem as they should be."

Becca turned the map so she could get a clear perspective of the various landmarks. "With Your Majesty's permission, I assume you want to know where the village was where the massacre took place?"

"Massacre?" The king's eyebrows rose almost to his hairline. He paused, then conceded the point. "Yes, I suppose it was. Do you know where the village was located?"

She pointed to the southern portion of Anacafria. "Here's the county of Guildenhall, and, as you know, Jeffries' lands are here." She moved her finger to the edge of the Obsidian Forest. "The village was here, in the southern portion of the forest. My friend, Nashotah, and I used to travel there as healers since the village didn't have one of their own."

The king's shoulders stiffened as he spoke angrily to the healer. "And you didn't see fit to tell me about this atrocity?"

Unnerved by the king's angry glare, Becca chose her next words carefully. "The only way to get word to Cafria was through a Royal Messenger, Sire. I didn't see one until I reached Merimeadow and found Herald Asrendian. She said she'd take the message for me, and I'd assumed she had."

The fanatical dedication of those assigned to the Messenger Service was legendary. All eyes turned to Marok to see if he could shed some light as to why the message hadn't gotten to the king. His face morphed into a mask of personal grief. Visibly pulling himself together, he looked directly into the king's eyes when he spoke. "Traders discovered Asrendian's body on the road that runs between Merimeadow and the ferry service at King's Crossing. We believe there may have been foul play, but —"

"Her *body*? You mean she was murdered? Everyone knows it's a death sentence for anyone who kills one of my messengers." Frustrated, Leopold turned to Jathez. "How is it that I'm not being told about the happenings in my own kingdom? We've worked years to organize the best system of communication this kingdom has ever known, and I'm still in the dark about major events."

Jathez looked to Marok for an explanation.

The herald let out a frustrated sigh. "When we notified the guard in Merimeadow, they began an investigation into her death. They may not have finished their inquiry yet, Sire, and might not have wanted to report to you until they had answers. I understand there was some unusual evidence at the scene. Some type of prints around her body, as though some animals had been fighting close by."

That startled both Becca and Bree. It sounded a little too much like what they'd experienced during the battle with the Teivaiedin. They both turned questioning eyes on Taklishim, who seemed just as unnerved as the two of them.

The shaman lifted a hand as he questioned Marok. "You say her name was Asrendian?"

When Marok nodded, the old man's eyes unfocused, and Becca knew he was speaking with his Spirit Guide, Acoma, the Mapînéh Fox from the Sixth Realm of Peritia. When he'd finished, a sadness washed over him as he addressed the king. "Your messenger, Asrendian, had a Coyote named Carn as her Guide. Carn was found several moons past staked out on the pathways between the Realms of Bendith and Lamina."

Out of respect, the king didn't immediately discount the older man's words. "And the significance of that is...what, exactly?"

Taklishim braced his hands on his knees, making himself more comfortable on the campstool he'd been provided. "There are many aspects of your world that you have chosen to disregard, King Leopold.

As the ruler of your people, you no longer have that luxury. The Spirit Realm has now visited death upon one of your own."

The old man once more turned to Marok. "There were no marks on the body of your friend." It was a statement rather than as a question.

Startled, Marok respectfully inclined his head to the shaman. "That is correct, Sir. It appeared as though she'd been galloping on the way to the ferry crossing when she simply fell from her horse." Sounding perplexed at the thought, he continued, "Her family breeds horses on the Silvermoor Steppes. Because of that, she'd been riding since before she could walk. Everyone on the Steppes is more comfortable on the back of a horse than on their own two feet. That's what didn't sit right with all of her friends. That's why it couldn't have simply been an accident." He turned to the king. "We knew she'd never simply fall off her horse, but we couldn't find any other reason for her to have ended up on dead the ground."

Darius, who'd been taught to listen carefully when attending meetings with his father, decided this would be a good time to get clarification on what Taklishim had intimated to his father. "You meant my father's Spirit Guide, didn't you? You meant he's ignored the Spirit Guides for too long. Why did you say that? What does it mean that the messenger's Spirit Guide was staked out on the pathways?"

The old man turned to the boy and held out his hand. "Come."

Darius stepped forward. At ten years old, he'd already had a good deal of training in bearing and deportment. He held himself straight as he stood in front of Taklishim, looking him in the eye with respect as he'd been taught a prince should acknowledge an elder statesman.

Taklishim also held out his hand to Kaiti, who hesitated before reluctantly inching her way forward. She stopped just out of reach of his weathered and gnarled fingers. It hadn't been so very long ago that simply being in the presence of the revered chieftain meant immediate death for her at the hands of the Shona.

Bree put her arm around Kaiti and edged her close enough for Taklishim to put his hand on her shoulder.

Denabi shimmered into existence next to Kaiti, and the old man smiled before acknowledging his old friend by running his fingers through the shining black fur between Denabi's muscular shoulder blades.

Most of the other people in the tent were oblivious to her presence, and they watched Taklishim's hand movements with incomprehension.

The prince, on the other hand, took in an excited breath and whispered, "Is there a Spirit Guide there? Is it my Guide? Is it a Silvermoor Leopard?"

Kaiti watched as Taklishim stroked Denabi's fur. She glanced over at the White Leopard lying patiently in the corner. Brékin was Darius' Spirit Guide, and Kaiti knew her friend could neither see nor hear her.

Becca turned and looked at Brékin as well. The prince desperately wanted to see his Guide, and she hadn't been able to help him. She'd spoken to Taklishim about the boy's questions and hoped he'd help him at some point during their trip.

"These are questions worthy of an honest answer, Young Cub." Taklishim glanced up at the king. "Is your father ready to hear the answers?"

All eyes looked to the king. Leopold had grown up in a household that despised the Shona. His father had tried his best to wipe them and their beliefs from the Anacafrian landscape, and yet, even as a young boy, Leopold had felt the presence of *something* always standing by his side during his greatest times of need.

When his father had been killed far away from the hill where Leopold and Bree were skirmishing during one of the battles of the Estian Wars, a voice in the back of his mind had told him he was now king. He'd known instinctively that the fate of his country suddenly rested squarely upon his shoulders. There hadn't been time to explain his premonition to Bree, so he'd shouted to her over the din of battle that his father had been struck down. Seconds later their position was overrun by a mounted force of Estian cavalry.

Bree hadn't hesitated, hadn't questioned his pronouncement. She desperately fought to protect her cousin, to the point of swinging her horse in front of his just as an arrow came flying at his chest. The arrow pierced her left shoulder, but she hadn't gone down until she'd rallied her guardsmen with the cry of "Protect the king! Protect King Leopold!"

With Bree's words echoing in their ears, the soldiers had fought like berserkers. Completely outnumbered, they'd managed to beat back the Estian forces until the Imperial Guard could make their way from where King Pries' body lay to fight at Leopold's side.

It had taken a royal proclamation, and the royal censure of several of the more stubborn nobles, but after the death of King Pries, Leopold finally put an end to the genocide begun by his father decades earlier. Unfortunately, he'd never been able to completely erase the prejudice King Pries had instilled in the hearts and minds of his people. As he watched his son standing in front of Taklishim, Leopold realized that perhaps it was Darius, rather than himself, who would one day reunite the two races.

As the silence lengthened, the king heard Kaiti gasp. He looked over in time to see Becca pull in a quick breath as well. He shuddered involuntarily as he felt a familiar, unseen presence in the room.

Becca blinked several times. The gray-blue eyes of a massive Teyvardian Mountain Goat regarded her with quiet amusement. With her heart pounding, she lowered her head, fighting the urge to kneel in front of the magnificent beast.

When Leopold's gaze met Taklishim's, there was an amused, knowing glint in the old man's eyes. The king glowered, not wanting to appear weak in front of the military leaders gathered in the tent. He motioned toward his son with an open hand. "Tell him what you will, and then we need to make our plans."

Taklishim nodded, then turned his attention to the young prince. Before he spoke, he glanced over his shoulder and asked Becca to translate for Kaiti. When she nodded, he began, "You asked if your father has ignored his Spirit Guide. I can only say that his Guide, Gari-ale, has spoken to him on many occasions." He smiled and looked at the king, "And on some occasions your father has actually taken heed." When the king shifted uncomfortably, Taklishim once again addressed the boy. "Now, he no longer has the luxury of ignorance. The Teivaiedin staked out and bled Carn, and as a result of Carn's death, your messenger, Asrendian, perished as well."

Marshal Sandresin, who'd been listening intently, asked, "What does that mean, exactly? That Carn was staked out and bled? I've never heard of someone dying because their Guide died, and I've done quite a bit of research on the subject of Shona lore. In fact, I'd always read that Spirit Guides don't die, they simply take on another apprentice when their current one passes on."

Marshal Andris Toker, who'd remained silent up to this point, chuckled. "Only you, Sandresin, only you."

Sandresin flashed a quick grin at his friend before turning back to Taklishim, who nodded before answering the young man. "You have not learned it because it has never happened in the history of my people. Have your studies told you of Morgrad and his followers being confined to Aecheron during the Peshár War?"

When Sandresin nodded, Taklishim continued, "Recently we discovered that Morgrad has somehow loosed the Teivaiedin—the antithesis to the Peshár, our Spirit Guides—from bonds thought to be eternal. And he has, through some unknown power or device, bound the Spirit Guides to their apprentice. When a Guide is killed and staked out by the Teivaiedin, the apprentice dies as well."

Marshal Toker shot an incredulous look at the king. "Your Majesty, you can't be taking all of this seriously." He looked back at Taklishim. "I mean no disrespect, Sir, but we are on the brink of war with Organdy, and I don't see how your spiritual beliefs can help us in any way." He once more addressed the king. "Sire, we're wasting valuable time here. Port Suliet is in my father's duchy. If Queen Desdamea lands, her forces will hit our shores first." He pointed to Salth on the map to emphasize his point.

King Leopold nodded and indicated Port Suliet, on the eastern shores of the Cascadian Sea. "I fully intend to mount a defense at Suliet, as I've already told your father. In fact, your considerable time spent at sea is one of the reasons I picked you to be one of my marshals. Your point is well taken. But, as our ally, I'll listen to everything Taklishim has to contribute."

He straightened and faced the young marshal. "One aspect of a good leader, Andris, is understanding that every small bit of information, no matter how insignificant it may seem at the time, just might make the difference between victory or defeat in battle. You'd do well to heed Sandresin's example and study cultures other than our own."

Andris had the grace to look chagrined. "You're right, of course, Your Majesty. My father has often chided me for my impatience."

The king's face softened as he regarded the young man. "I'm not chiding you, Andris. You're a grown man, albeit not yet thirty, and I value your opinion. If I didn't, you wouldn't be here."

Leopold turned back to Taklishim. "So, what you're saying, is that you believe Asrendian's death is a direct result of what happened to her Spirit Guide?"

Bree spoke up. "That's what I've been worrying about these last few weeks, Sire. We may be fighting a battle on two fronts. And who knows? If the Teivaiedin actually do exist..."

She turned to Marshal Toker, "and after what happened at the Battle of the Seven Realms, I now believe they do, then we'll be hard pressed to address both enemies at the same time."

Toker, who was listening more intently now, nodded, apparently at least trying to see his world from a different perspective.

Bree continued, "I've been wondering if what Desdamea is doing could very well be a direct result of the Teivaiedin's influence. The two could possibly be connected somehow."

When Bree finished speaking, Leopold once again addressed the young man. "What's your opinion, Andris?"

The marshal thought a minute. He glanced around, taking in the Shona warriors, the herald, the duchess, the lord commander and his fellow marshals. His eyes wandered down to his sword hilt where he rested his gloved hand. Finally, he looked up at his king. "I can't say I believe in Spirit Guides or the Teivaiedin, Your Majesty, but I can't ignore the facts surrounding Asrendian's death either. I knew her well. She apprenticed with our master herald in Salth. While there, she gave riding lessons to my father and he, in turn, mandated that every member of our family take lessons from her as well. I've seen her ride over terrain without a saddle that would have unseated any one of us, and she never even came close to falling off. It's that fact, and only that fact, that gives me pause."

It seemed as though he meant to say more, and the king encouraged him. "And..."

"And, without a reason for her to fall from her horse, short of an arrow through her eye or a garrote rope tied across the trail, well, the chief's words have given me a lot to think about."

Everyone looked to Taklishim whose hands rested quietly in his lap. He brought one gnarled finger to his ear and then spoke directly to Andris, "It is good that you listen. You must hear this as well. This child," He pointed to Kaiti first, then paused and pointed to the prince, "and the king's son, have a shared destiny." He caught and held Toker's gaze. "Whether you believe or whether you choose to deny your Guide, above all else, you must protect these two children. Your destiny is caught up in theirs. Your life must be pledged to them, even more than it is pledged to your king."

Marshal Toker sputtered, subconsciously taking a small step back from the Shaman, his incredulous stare sweeping the room, apparently searching for a familiar halyard to brace himself against in these unfamiliar seas.

Bree understood his reaction. As a marshal, Toker might have command of a thousand or more troops, all of them sworn to the crown. His oath to Leopold was sacrosanct, and he'd never allow anything to alter that fact.

His uneasy gaze finally came to rest upon the king, who simply shrugged, "I'm sure he doesn't mean in this instant, Andris. I'm willing to say that when the time comes for Taklishim's words to bear fruit, there will be no question as to your loyalties or to the direction you must take. All I ask is that you take heed and remember his advice should the time come for you to act. Remember what I said a few minutes ago—any one insignificant piece of information might mean the difference between victory or defeat." He turned and leaned over the table with the maps. "Now, let's take a look at our defenses, shall we?"

Taklishim's face had grown gray from fatigue and he motioned to Tisneé, letting him know he was ready to return to his tent. The young warrior helped the old man to his feet and supported him as they left.

Becca watched him go and then asked Bree, "Do you want me to take Kaiti and get her something to eat? I'm willing to bet she's nearly dead from starvation since you usually forget to eat nine meals out of ten."

Bree realized quite a few candlemarks had passed since they'd last eaten. "Thanks. And ask Eavan to bring me something as well." She joined the men around the map before remembering her earlier conversation with the arms master. "Oh, and Kalsik is going to take her to the weapons smith tonight to get her measured for a practice sword."

Ushering Kaiti out of the tent, Becca answered over her shoulder. "I'll be sure to deliver her into his very capable hands." With that, she dropped the tent flap in place and left them to their strategy session.

CHAPTER 4

The following day, the king's army steadily grew as they made their way to King's City. When Leopold had first heard the rumors that Desdamea was gathering her forces, he'd put out a call for each of his dukes to supply half the number of soldiers needed for a full-scale war.

Since then, troops from Thadon, Marblefort Downs and Deerford had been moving into the areas surrounding King's City. These weren't the regular troops assigned to the Queen's Battalions or to Huntington's Cavalry. They were men and women who trained as local militia, ready at a moment's notice to take up arms whenever the king required their duke to supply ready troops.

The lower classes considered duty in the militia a privilege, primarily because every Duchy gave three copper rions per day to the families of the soldiers away fighting for the Kingdom. The dukes also provided a weapons instructor for every hamlet and village within their domain.

Members of the militia were required to be proficient with the sword and one other weapon of their choice, be it throwing knives, pole-ax, crossbow (although very few of the peasants could afford one), short bow, halberd or mace.

For the last several candlemarks, the king and his troops had made good time through the Forest of Aeval. Jathez had called a halt near a clearing not far from the town of Tessarod, and after everyone had dismounted and claimed a place to rest, legions of cooks' helpers no older than ten fanned out among the ranks handing out hunks of bread and cheese.

Once everyone had been served, a young noble appeared from the midst of the surrounding forest and strode over to where the king sat with his back against a tree. The man held the upper arm of a woman whose hands were bound behind her back. It seemed the entire town followed in his wake. When they reached the king, everyone, including the prisoner, bowed respectfully.

Bree, who sat next to the king, studied the woman. She wore the leather trews and tunic of a trapper, light brown and cleaner than Bree would have expected. The fabric pulled tightly against muscular arms and the tops of her dark brown boots rose to just below her knees. She wore her thick, black hair short and straight and as she rose from her bow, the letter C burned into the upper portion of her right cheek startled everyone into silence.

The king set his cup of mead on the ground and rose. He rested his hand on his sword hilt while he waited for the young nobleman to speak.

Bree set her plate down and stood as well.

Curious about the newcomers, soldiers from throughout the camp began to gather, and a crowd quickly formed a circle around the little group.

The nobleman nervously cleared his throat. "Your Majesty, I'm Baron Humphries from the Barony at Tessarod."

The king nodded. "I was sorry to hear of the death of your father. He was a good man."

The baron's face fell into a brief mask of grief. "Thank you, Sire. My mother, brothers and I still mourn his loss. By the time I'd gotten to King's City to swear my allegiance to Your Majesty, you had already left for Orinshire." He bowed slightly to Bree. "I'm pleased to see Your Grace looking so well."

Bree acknowledged his regard with a slight nod.

Humphries put his hand on the prisoner's back and pushed her forward a step. "Sire, this woman came into Tessarod several days ago asking to be sent to King's City. She intended to request a royal audience. I knew you were coming through Tessarod after visiting the duchess at Orinshire, and I kept her in the village smokehouse until your arrival."

Harsh whispering had begun among the soldiers. An angry glare from Jathez silenced them.

The king waited several moments before addressing the woman. "You've been branded with the mark of a coward. According to the laws of the kingdom, I should have you beaten to within an inch of your life for daring to enter one of my cities and then tie you out for the wolves to feed on your carcass. What possible motive can you have to risk your life to come speak to me?"

The woman squared her shoulders. "I have no reason for your mercy, Your Majesty, unless you would spare the lives of these guards as well." The woman motioned to the ones guarding her with her chin.

The king pulled his eyebrows low. "These soldiers? Explain yourself."

"Your guards are good people. Each with perhaps a mother or father, brother, sister, wife, husband or children. I'll not go without a fight, and one, or all of your guards who stand against me will die. I'd rather not see that happen."

The king studied this strange woman.

Bree stepped up next to him. She was curious now, more so because the woman spoke with the accent of an educated Estian citizen instead of with the common guttural tongue she expected. "Why were you branded a coward?"

The woman met Bree's gaze with a steady strength in her eyes. "I was an officer in the Estian 7th cavalry. A year ago, when we were fighting to keep Organdy from crossing into Estia, my regiment fought a detachment of their Black Mountaineers. In the end, we routed them. I had killed their constable during the battle and once the fighting ended, the rest of his soldiers, some fifty that were left, laid down their weapons and knelt before me. I told one of my seconds to take them prisoner. Just as he and his squad began to comply, the constable in charge of our regiment rode up and ordered me to execute those who were left alive."

A shocked gasp rippled through the crowd. Bree felt her stomach clench and noticed Jathez' jaw tighten in anger. Honor dictated that defeated enemy soldiers be taken prisoner and either ransomed or offered asylum. If they refuse to change their allegiance, they are held in the king's prisons until the end of the hostilities. Knowing how Desdamea's troops felt about her, Bree guessed every one of them would beg for asylum and would take any position offered in the Estian armies.

The woman turned her attention from Bree to the king. "I refused to kill men and women who surrendered to me with honor. When I refused, the constable stepped forward to kill them himself. I stood between him and the prisoners and drew my weapon. My second and seven of my people drew their weapons and came to stand beside me. All of us were ready to defend the prisoners with our own lives if necessary."

Glancing around, Bree noticed several people nodding as they listened to the story.

The woman continued her tale. "At that point, sub-commander Shoan arrived. He is an honorable man with generations of soldiering in his blood. When he saw what the constable was about to do, he ordered the prisoners taken away. However, because I had disobeyed a direct order and had drawn a weapon against my superior, sub-commander Shoan felt he had no choice but to allow the constable to brand me and the eight who stood by my side."

Murmuring began among the ranks as the king looked at her through hooded eyes. It was an expression his people knew well. He was a fair man who held his innermost thoughts to himself until he decided upon a course of action. "What of the other eight?"

The woman's eyes changed from calm azure to ice in the time it took the king to finish his words. "One of my best archers was stoned to death at the first town he came to." She leveled her gaze on the king. "I assure you, his death was avenged." She paused, waiting for that to sink in. "Another has become a highwayman in Organdy."

When she didn't continue, Jathez asked what was on everyone's minds. "That leaves six others..."

"Yes, it does. My people are expert bowmen who are watching these proceedings with great interest."

The soldiers guarding the woman looked around nervously.

Rocca, who was standing off to the side, laid his hand on the hilt of his sword and stepped in front of the king. Two others of the Imperial Guard took up positions at his back, facing outward toward the forest.

The woman shook her head. "You don't have to worry that we'd harm your king. He has a reputation as that of a good, honest man, which..." She shrugged, lifting her eyebrows to emphasize her point, "Is hard to come by in the way of kings. I would defend him with my life if needs be. But these men and women," She indicated the guards to either side of her, "they're soldiers who understand the ways of battle. My people won't hesitate to fire on them if that's what it takes to keep my head on my shoulders."

The king's expression darkened. "I don't take threats to my guards lightly. Do so again and your life is forfeit. Now, I ask you again. Tell me why I should spare your life."

The woman lowered her head, thinking. After a few moments she brought her chin up and looked directly into his eyes. "Because I'm tired of being an outcast among my people who claim to hold honor and the knight's code above all else. What my soldiers and I did was right, and I stand by our actions to this day. We came to Anacafria because we knew about you and your kingdom. You not only hold honor in high regard, but you live what you believe. These guards," She turned first to look at the man on her right, and then to the woman on her left. "they've treated me fairly. When your townspeople saw my scar, they didn't spit in my face nor throw rocks at my back. They surrounded me, asked me to wait, and then called for the baron and his guards."

Her face softened as she looked at the young man who'd had to assume the title of baron at much too young an age. "Even though he locked me up, he fed me and saw to it that I was warm at night." She fell silent a moment, then knelt before the king and bowed her head.

"I put my life, the lives of my soldiers, and, more importantly, our honor in your hands."

Leopold stood quietly a moment, thinking. Those around the circle waited expectantly to see what he would do. The guards on either side of the woman still scanned the tree lines looking for telltale signs of archers.

Bree studied the trees as well. When she'd commanded Huntington's Cavalry, she'd faced their Estian counterparts on many, many occasions. The precision of their archers had led her to set the archery standards for her own riders twice as high as they'd been before.

Leopold turned and strode toward the back of one of the wagons. As he did so, he signaled for Bree and Jathez to join him. Darius quietly came and stood nearby, not sure if he was to be included in the conversation as well.

The king turned his back on the prisoner and her guards and spoke quietly. "Opinions?"

Bree looked to Jathez, who shook his head. "I don't know, Sire. There's a reason all of the kingdoms are so hard on those who've been branded. If we allow leniency in one case, I'm afraid it might cause others to expect leniency as well."

Leopold massaged the back of his neck. "On the other hand, if someone is wrongfully branded, is it right to continue to allow others to treat them as an outcast? A pariah? To allow them to be reviled everywhere they show their face?" He paused. "But then again, how do we know she's telling the truth? Maybe she and her followers did commit treason or extreme cowardice and were rightfully branded."

Bree had an idea. "One of the camp workers who came with us from Orinshire was a refugee from Estia. I think he belonged to an Estian soldier or some such thing. I don't remember why, but about nine months ago he showed up at Orinshire and asked for asylum. I remember Ellsworth writing me about it while I was at my steading. All the reports I've gotten from him say the boy seems a good, honest lad." She turned and called for Becca, who'd remained seated on the back of Taklishim's wagon.

The healer jumped down and strode quickly over them.

"I think you were at Orinshire getting supplies when that man—

actually he was more of a boy at the time—came from Estia asking for asylum, right?"

Becca nodded. "I was. I remember him well. He walked with a limp because he'd been knifed in the thigh as he was trying to slip off the ship he'd stowed away on. He had a particularly nasty infection. If he hadn't come to us when he did, he'd have been dead in a matter of days."

She paused, trying to recall more details about the boy. "He also had some bad scarring on his back. He told me he'd been bought by a man who beat him more often than he fed him. He followed me around like a puppy after I treated him. I think he works for Kalsik now, tending his and the prince's weapons. An unofficial squire, more or less."

Darius spoke up excitedly. "Rand? I'll go get him!" He turned, obviously intending to run get the young man when Leopold laid a hand his shoulder.

The king leaned down and spoke softly in the boy's ear. "Easy lad. All eyes are on you, especially at this particular moment. Walk calmly like the dignified prince I've taught you to be, not like some camp hellion racing through the ranks making a fool of himself. Now," He patted the boy on the back. "Go get the young Estian and bring him here."

Knowing his enthusiasm had once again almost betrayed him, Darius took a second to compose himself before calmly turning and walking through a gap that opened in the circle of onlookers as he approached.

Nordin followed, and interestingly enough, to Bree anyway, a white Silvermoor Leopard followed him as well. "Is that Darius' Guide?"

Becca, who'd also been watching the Leopard, turned to Bree. "It is. Her name's Brékin. For some reason she's been staying close to him lately. I've asked Garan why, but he just says it's necessary right now."

The piercing gaze the king turned on Becca was a little unnerving. As a healer assigned directly to Bree during the Estian Wars, she'd been around royalty enough to know it was much better to remain in the background than to attract unwanted attention.

Leopold glanced toward his son's retreating back. "What exactly does 'it's necessary' mean? And who is Garan?"

The White Wolf materialized in front of Becca, craning his head over his shoulder to look at her while the rest of his body faced the king. *Tell him I'm the hero of the Battle of the Seven Realms.* His tongue lolled to the side of his mouth and his eyes sparkled playfully.

Becca and Bree both snorted.

The king lowered his eyelids a fraction. "Excuse me? Did I say something amusing?"

Becca shook her head. "No Sire. Garan is my slightly egocentric Spirit Guide. He's a White Wolf."

Leopold shifted and rested his hand on the hilt of his sword. Lately, after Bree's experience, he'd begun to believe in the possible existence of the Spirit Guides, and he didn't trust a timber wolf not to rip his throat out if given half the chance.

Garan let out an amused yelp. *He looks worried Sheah. Maybe he's beginning to come around after all if he thinks the big bad Wolf is going to eat him.*

The king spoke to Bree. "Why can you see him, and I can't?"

Shrugging, Bree pointed into the wagon where Taklishim lay under a pile of furs, apparently napping. "I have no idea. You might want to talk to him about that."

Lowering his voice to a whisper, Leopold leaned in so the crowd of onlookers wouldn't hear him. "What did he mean 'it's necessary'? If Darius is in danger, I need to know so I can increase his guard."

What I meant was, Denabi feels it is imperative that the boy awaken to Brékin, and she ordered her to remain close by as much as she can. Denabi's not sure why, but after a couple thousand years of raising apprentices she's developed a sixth sense about such things. Sometimes, if the Spirit Guide remains near their apprentice, he or she gradually becomes aware of another presence in their immediate vicinity. It's the first step in the bonding process.

He swung his head around and studied the king. *She thinks the king will awaken as well, but his guide is needed on the pathways right now and can't remain as close as Brékin remains to the boy.*

Becca finished repeating what Garan had told them just as Darius walked up with a short, dark-skinned lad following him. The two boys stopped in front of the king.

Darius' companion snatched a knitted cap off his head, revealing an unruly mop of ruddy brown hair that fell forward over his face as he sketched an awkward bow. When he straightened, he nervously licked his heavy lips, glancing up at Bree before quickly lowering his head again.

Bree sensed his discomfort and made an attempt to reassure the boy. "King Leopold, may I introduce Rand, one of the most loyal citizens of Danforth."

Relief washed over Rand and some semblance of color returned to his face.

The king knew how disconcerting it could be for peasants to be in his presence, so he decided to get right to the point. "You're from Estia?"

"Arr, that I be."

"And you worked for a soldier in the Estian army?"

Rand shuffled his feet and became very interested in some nearby dirt clods. "Arr. Wey, ah worked fo' ta cook who made scran fo' ta soldiers."

"Do you remember hearing about an incident where some Orgundian soldiers were captured by a squadron of Estian cavalry, and something very unusual happened?"

The boy's face lifted and once again relief spread across his features. "Ah 'member."

Jathez spoke up then. "I remember, *Your Majesty*."

The blush started at the boy's neck and rose to the tips of his ears. "Ah member, Yah Majesty." He bowed again, this time keeping his eyes on the ground when he straightened.

Leopold caught Jathez' gaze and shook his head slightly. It was difficult enough getting something out of a boy like this without Jathez intimidating him.

Jathez scowled and nodded his understanding.

The king continued his questioning. "Tell me what you know."

The boy swiped his hand under his nose before answering. "I was worken fer Migi. Ee was ta cook me da sold me ter. Ee cooked fer ta soldiers."

The king looked at Bree who shrugged. She'd thought a soldier had owned him, but she was happy she'd remembered the boy at all, let alone recall the details correctly.

Completely unaware of their brief exchange, the boy continued, "Ee come back laughen 'un day. Said he'd just seen an uppity officer get 'er due." He looked up then, his eyes wide. "She uz branded!"

"Do you know why?"

He nodded. "Migi tot it were funny, but I knowed ta boy that worked fer 'er. Fin said she uz protecten sum prisners frum getten kilt by 'er higher up." Looking to Jathez for guidance, he asked, "Wull I be fash if I say what me skip said abart 'er higher up? It's not real gud abart him, an ee's a higher up 'n all."

Shaking his head, Jathez motioned for the boy to continue.

Rand took a breath. "Me skip said 'er higher up were bad news. He said ta lady were in the roight of it."

Darius piped up. "He means his friend. He calls a friend his skip."

The king, who understood most dialects, including peasant, nodded. "Would you recognize the officer if you saw her again?"

The boy shook his head, thoughtfully. "I don' think so. I niver got round ta sodiers much. Ol' Migi kept me scrubbin' pots b'hine ta cook wagons."

Kalsik pushed his way through the circle of onlookers. He stepped up next to the boy and after bowing, indicated Rand with a slight wave of his hand. "Is there a problem I can help with, Sire? The boy works for me. One of the lads said Darius had come to get him for you."

Leopold sighed. "No problem, Kalsik. Rand was giving us some information on an incident that happened when he lived in Estia." He turned and spoke to Rand. "Thank you, Rand. You may return to your duties now."

Rand started to turn, then at the last minute remembered he was supposed to bow. He bent at the waist, and then, from the bent over position, awkwardly looked up at Jathez before addressing the king, "Arr, Yah Majesty."

As he and Kalsik left, the king glanced around, lowering his voice so only Bree and Jathez would hear. "Well, that pretty much confirms what the woman said. In good conscience, I can't turn her out, Jathez. Bree, what's your opinion?"

Bree crossed her arms, slowly tapping her finger on her tunic as she thought about what the woman had said. "I believe her, Leo. If you'll allow it, I'll take her and her soldiers into one of my battalions. I'll keep a close watch on them to make sure they're not spies, and if they prove to be cowards, I'll brand their other cheek myself."

Relieved, the king took hold of Bree's arm. She'd just handed him an out, and he gratefully accepted. "I'll allow it. Thank you, Cousin."

Bree gave him a wolfish grin. "It doesn't come without a price."

The side of the king's mouth quirked into a half smile. "I didn't think so. So, tell me what I owe you this time."

"I'd like to have Sandresin as one of my marshals."

"Of course. But I want to keep him and Andris Toker under the same lord, and I know Jathez wanted to have Aiden Tulane and Jeffries working for him." He shrugged at Jathez. "I guess we'll have to find you another marshal since I took Jeffries out of the picture, but we'll discuss that later."

The four of them walked back to where the baron and his prisoner waited. Bree studied the crowd as they returned. Some stared at the king, but many of them glared suspiciously at the woman, who bore the brand most reviled by every peasant, freeman, noble and most importantly, every soldier throughout the land.

When her gaze came back to the woman, she realized she'd been under scrutiny as well. She admired the calm demeanor the prisoner displayed, despite the fact that her life was on the line. Once again, Bree admired the high cheekbones and straight, black hair. She wondered if some of the Shona who'd fled across the Cascadian Sea had married into the woman's bloodline.

When the king began to speak, the whispers that had begun during their conference faded into silence. "Give me your name."

The woman lifted her chin and gave her name proudly. "Verigo Liris Estia."

Bree was fairly certain only a few in the crowd knew what the woman had just implied, but when she looked at the king, it was obvious he did. In the Estian tradition, a person has two first names, followed by the name of the town or city where they were born. The nobility always has their country's name as the last, instead of their city. The primary first name denotes the person's status in their clan and the second is generally the name of a deceased family member. If someone referred to a person in a formal setting, all three names would be used. If the gathering or meeting was informal, the second name was used.

Leopold blinked once, then, for a brief moment, returned Bree's gaze. They'd known each other since childhood, and words weren't always necessary for them to communicate. The king lifted his eyebrow, and she responded by opening her eyes a little wider. Translated, the exchange meant, "Did you know?" to which Bree had replied, "Hardly."

Bree's Spirit Guide, Ebi suddenly appeared at her side. *Well, well, well. Isn't this interesting. You know the Estians don't take a person's nobility into account when they serve in the military. If they commit a transgression, as long as they aren't the king or queen, they're treated just like any other soldier.* Not taking her eyes off the woman, the Badger waddled toward Taklishim's wagon.

The woman's eyes tracked the Badger as she moved.

This brought the Guide up short. *And you can see and hear me as well, can't you?*

The slight nod the woman gave convinced Bree of her Shona heritage. Legend had it that the goddess Aevala only gave her Spirit Guides to the inhabitants of Anacafria. So how did Shona blood get into the Estian royal bloodlines so soon after Pries began his purge?

Kaiti's Guide Denabi appeared as well. Ebi motioned to the woman with a lift of her chin. *Sorry to pull you out of the realms, Dens, but this is important. This woman's name is...Verigo Liris Estia, and she can see and hear us.*

Denabi's gaze took in the woman and the guards, as well as the scar that stood out prominently on her right cheek. She stepped forward and addressed the prisoner. *Where is your Guide?*

As she spoke, a Fisher Cat came striding out of the forest. He was taller than most, with his shoulders coming to about knee height on a human. He walked to the woman's side before turning and facing Denabi. *Hello, Denabi.* He glanced at the Badger. *Ebi.*

Denabi stepped forward and touched noses with him before turning and addressing Bree. *I hope Leopold knows he'd better keep the significance of her name to himself. Liris was the Estian queen two generations ago. Verigo means she's the niece of the current king.*

Bree silently agreed and was relieved when Leopold continued as though the name meant nothing to him. "Verigo Liris Estia. You are correct when you say I hold honor in high regard. The boy, Rand, formally from Estia, has verified your story. I believe you were acting with honor when you drew your weapon to defend the prisoners, and the eight soldiers who stood at your side, knowing their fate, displayed the loyalty I hold dear among my own fighting men and women. As ruler of Anacafria, I thereby rescind your disgrace and welcome you and your people into my country. If any of you wish to serve me in a military capacity, the Duchess Aurelia Makena has agreed to sponsor you among her troops."

Whooping and cheering came from the trees as several armed bowmen leapt from their concealment among the branches and boughs. A man and a woman hugged one another while three other men pounded each other on the back.

A lone archer jumped down from one of the higher branches, strode through the circle of Anacafrian soldiers and knelt before the king. He laid his crossbow and arrows at the king's feet, drew his belt knife and held it point first to his breast. "I am Andrin Magnus Estia, former knight of the Estian court. I swear my fealty to you and serve as you see fit."

At the king's nod, the guard to the right of the woman drew his own knife and cut her bonds. When she was free, she also stepped forward and knelt. She quietly addressed the kneeling man out of the side of her mouth. "Always have to be first, don't you, Magnus?"

Leopold held back a smile and took the hilt of the proffered knife.

To Bree's surprise, Jathez stepped forward and offered Liris his own dirk since Baron Humphries had seen fit to confiscate hers.

Liris thanked him and placed the tip of the dirk over her heart. There were more similarities than differences in the oaths of each county, and Bree listened with interest to the Estian version as the two spoke their vows.

Liris glanced out of the corner of her eye at Magnus to see if he wanted to give the oath first.

He shook his head, a slight grin pulling up the corners of his mouth.

She looked up at Leopold who took hold of the hilt of her knife with his free hand. She spoke clearly, with only a hint of an Estian accent. "My life for your life, my blood for your blood, my death for your honor. I will stand strong and true in defense of your kingdom and in defense of your lineage. My sword will defend you, my words will honor you, and my will shall be obedient to your command. I will defend the defenseless, speak only the truth, and choose loyalty to my monarch over riches and approbation. This I do swear and will uphold for as long as there is breath in my body."

When Magnus repeated the oath, the king accepted their pledge and recited his oath back to them.

While all this was happening, Bree once again studied the crowd. Many of the glares were replaced with puzzled looks. Common soldiers didn't kneel before the king and give their oaths. In fact, the five who'd held back while Liris and Magnus took their oath now walked forward, bowed once to the king, and then knelt behind the woman and waited.

Bree heard people talking amongst themselves, questioning each other as to the possible meaning behind Liris and Magnus swearing as though they were noble knights of the realm. Everyone quieted when the king held up his hand for silence.

"The seven of you are now free Anacafrians and as such will have documents to carry with you stipulating that fact. If you choose to serve as soldiers, I must demand one," Leopold looked pained at what he had to say. "sacrifice on your part. You must allow one more scar on your cheek. A single line next to the open end of your C, thereby turning your disgrace as a coward into your pride as a defender."

Bree blanched. Leopold's solution was the only way any of them would be accepted into the fighting ranks. No one wanted to have a branded coward guarding their backs, even if the branding was in error. With the brilliant idea of replacing the c with a d, he'd solved that problem as well. She watched Liris, wondering if she would accept the king's conditions.

Without hesitation, Liris nodded. "I accept."

As if they'd been waiting for her decision, Magnus and the other five said in unison. "I accept."

Bree saw Liris glance at the Fisher Cat and could tell by the hackles on the animal's back that he was not in the least bit pleased. She understood his anger. Being seared by a hot iron was not only excruciatingly painful, it could also result in a lethal infection if something were to go wrong with the process.

All three Spirit Guides disappeared as quickly and as unexpectedly as they'd arrived. Leopold ordered Jathez to arrange accommodations and supplies for Liris and her people. Jathez turned to Cameron, who nodded once before ushering the seven newcomers away from the immediate area.

CHAPTER 5

Two days later, after a couple of long, hard days of travel, Kaiti reluctantly followed Tisneé through camp. He'd told her Taklishim wanted to speak with her, which caused her insides to clench with dread. Dragging her feet through the dust that poofed up with each of her tentative steps, she fell further and further behind until Tisneé finally noticed she was no longer at his side.

When he glanced back, he noticed her unhappy look and waited for her to catch up.

Kaiti slowed her pace even more.

Tisneé knelt so he could look the little girl in the eyes. He'd always liked the Spirit Child and had often taken her food or offered her a blanket on particularly cold nights.

It wasn't reasonable that he should feel differently about her than how most of the members of his tribe felt. She'd killed his brother after all. But his brother had killed her family first, and in his mind, the child had been justified in what she'd done. No one could prove she'd slipped into the warriors' tents at night and slit their throats or added poison to their drinks. But both he, and the healer Nashotah, knew in their hearts that Katie had been the one to skillfully avenge the deaths of her loved ones.

Kaiti let out a long sigh.

He lifted her chin with one finger until she looked him directly in the eyes. "Your feet seem to be hurting you. Shall I carry you the rest of the way?" He grinned because they both knew only infants needed to be carried.

Kaiti saw the twinkle in his eyes and smiled shyly.

"So...why so sad? Is the Badger giving you a hard time?"

When Kaiti shook her head, he asked, "Then something else is bothering you. Will you tell me what it is?"

Kaiti glanced nervously at Taklishim's tent.

Tisneé immediately understood. "He only wants to talk with you, and I think he intends to begin teaching you. There are customs and ideas I'll bet you're curious about, aren't there?"

Nodding once, Kaiti asked, "What if I can't learn what he teaches?"

The big warrior gave her question some thought before answering. "Well, whether you learn his lessons or not, you have a unique gift that no one else in all the Shona lands has ever had. I think because of that, it's important for you to at least try. And if you fail," He shrugged. "you will still be able to hold your head up knowing you did your best for the Shona, the Deaf Ones, and the Spirit Guides."

The Shona called the Anacafrians the Deaf Ones, because most of them had lost the ability to see or hear their Spirit Guides. Tisneé put his hand on her shoulder. "I guess that sounds like an awful lot resting on the shoulders of a nine-year-old, doesn't it? I think your friend Darius feels the same weight resting upon him. Are you making progress learning his language?"

"Shimaa teaches me while we ride, but their words are so strange. It's hard to say them right."

The way she said "their words" bothered Tisneé. He loved being Shona and was proud of his ancestors and their traditions. How many times had he and his friends sat around a tribal fire listening to Taklishim or Taima as they spoke of great battles or of heroic deeds done long ago by Spirit Guides and their apprentices?

Once more, shame washed over him as he thought about what his brother had done to this little girl. He hadn't only taken her family, he'd taken her identity as well. She was neither Shona nor Anacafrian.

A screech sounded in the sky above them, and he looked up to see Azeel. He held out his arm and the steel colored raptor swooped low before gliding up and landing gracefully on his forearm.

The Shengali Hawk tilted his black head to the side as he spoke. *Instead of no culture, she is part of three.* He turned intense eyes on Kaiti who immediately lowered her gaze. He spoke directly to her. *Old habits die hard, little cub, but you must believe in who you are. Break the habit of averting your eyes and fading into the background. Meet the gaze of everyone you meet, with the exception of the king, whether they are Shona, Anacafrian or Spirit Guide. You have learned extreme humility, now you must embrace all of the many aspects of a prideful mind. When you grow to be a full Leopardess, the balance will be somewhere in between.*

Kaiti brought her eyes up and stared into his, then squared her sagging shoulders, giving her an additional two inches along with a much-needed boost to her flagging confidence. Turning toward the Shona tent, she strode, perhaps not boldly, but determinedly, over to it and ducked under the animal skin covering.

Taklishim sat propped against a log in front of a small fire. His face lit with pleasure when she entered, bolstering her confidence even more.

Tisneé followed her in. He motioned toward Kaiti and smiled. "I've brought the cub, Honored Father. I promised the healer I'd help her gather some herbs she needs from the woods. Do you need anything more before I go?"

"You could ask her to find some warrow root for my aching bones. Aevala allowed me to remain in this Realm but she neglected to provide me with a body that doesn't ache more and more with each passing day." He motioned to Kaiti. "What do you think Panther Cub? Maybe I should have remembered to ask Aevala for a thirty-year-old body when I asked whether I could stay, hmmm?"

Kaiti giggled.

Tisneé took that as his cue that she was comfortable enough for him to leave. He ducked back out of the tent.

When the flap dropped, she asked timidly, "Do you have the moss from under the roots of the Kaisa Tree? Adené showed me how to crush it and boil it in water to ease Breah's aches."

Taklishim scrunched his nose and shook his head. "No, Little Cub. I'd rather fight with the goddess over a new body than drink that concoction Adené brews. It works wonders, but it tastes like someone crushed up a dung beetle and poured the powder into a cup of bog water." He raised his eyebrows. "Have you ever tasted a dung beetle?"

Kaiti laughed out loud, then quickly covered her mouth, leaving only her smiling eyes peeking out over her fingers. She lowered her hand and spoke loud enough for old ears to hear. "That's almost exactly what Breah said after she took a big gulp and threw the cup at Adené." As Kaiti recounted the scene, Denabi appeared in the corner of the tent. The Panther padded close to the fire and lay down, crossing one paw over the other in her characteristic way.

Taklishim placed his hand on her shoulder. "Your arrival could not have been better timed, my friend. We have much work to accomplish in a very short time."

Denabi rubbed her head against his shoulder in greeting. *Have you discussed anything with her yet?*

Shaking his head, he brought his gaze up to meet Kaiti's. "We are going on a journey tonight, Little Cub."

Kaiti's eyebrows came down low over her eyes. "Who?"

Denabi answered quietly. *I will be with you the entire time. Nothing will harm you. Taklishim will be with us as well.*

"Where are we going? Does Shimaa know? Will she come with us?"

Your mother cannot come where we go. There is much happening along the pathways and in the other realms. Battles are being fought, and we find ourselves falling to an enemy we cannot see.

Kaiti jumped to her feet, eyes wide with fear and disbelief. "No!" Her panicked gaze flew between the Shaman and her Spirit Guide. "I can't! I'll die! They'll kill me for going there! I can't!" She turned to run from the tent, but Garan materialized in the opening before she reached it.

Hey there, Kitten. Denabi doesn't know it yet, but I'm coming too.

Ebi, Bree's Guide, materialized as well. *As am I.* She looked around the confines of the little tent. *It's getting a little crowded in here, don't you think?*

Taklishim chuckled and motioned for Kaiti to join him once again by the fire. "No one is going to kill you, Little Cub. While these brave and honorable Guides are welcome to meet us on the pathways, there's really no need on tonight's journey. Our trips will not be long at first, as we will simply be training and learning. There will be no battles, and you have nothing to fear."

"But the Shona! They'll kill me for walking the pathways. I can't!"

Garan growled low in his throat. *I should have bitten some heads off in Dahana's camp when I had the chance.*

No one spoke as Taklishim once again motioned for Kaiti to sit. When she hesitantly lowered herself to the ground, he settled further into the blanket he wore around his shoulders. "You had many lessons to learn in Dahana's camp. Who can guess the reasons behind Aevala's plans for our lives? She has given you a rare and beautiful gift. You alone can see the Teivaiedin, and great deeds will be required of you. For that purpose, you need an uncommon strength. A strength that an ordinary childhood would not have given you. As far as the Shona, they will touch no one under my protection, and you, I protect most of all."

He indicated Ebi and Garan with his hands opened wide. "There will come a time when you are needed, my friends, but this is not that time."

Garan stepped over and pushed his nose under Kaiti's chin, lifting it slightly, then pulling away. *I will be where you need me, whenever you need me.* With that, he faded into the other realms.

When Ebi waddled over, Kaiti turned to her. "Will you tell Shimaa? She needs to know."

Easy, Child. Taklishim's already spoken to her. She's not happy about your travels, but she trusts our Shaman and has given her permission. She lifted her shoulders in a Badger's equivalent of a shrug. *And she threatened to skin me and hang my pelt on her wall if anything happens to you.* She bared her teeth and clacked them together as she waddled out of the tent. *I'd like to see her try...*

Three pairs of eyes watched the rippling waves of fur-covered fat on her backside as she disappeared through the opening. Denabi blinked, shaking her head in admiration. *She may be well-padded, but there's no one fiercer than she throughout all the Realms.*

Taklishim reached into a pouch on his belt, pinched a small amount of herb and sprinkled it into the orange flames. When he finished, he settled back against the log. "Now, Little Cub. Move over here next to me and we will begin."

Kaiti pushed up onto her knees and swiveled around until she was sitting just as she'd been instructed. She wasn't happy about this new turn of events, but if the Guides were being attacked by the Teivaiedin on the pathways, and if she could somehow help them, she realized she should at least give it a try.

Taklishim's Spirit Guide, Acoma, materialized and immediately curled up on the furs next to the Shaman's legs. His Amber-gold eyes took in his surroundings before coming to rest on Kaiti. Never loquacious, he simply met her gaze with a steady one of his own.

Taklishim rested his hand on the Fox's back in a familiar gesture and began his instructions. "Now, just as I am unable to walk the pathways without Acoma, you, too, will need the assistance of Denabi during your journeys. I want you to open yourself up completely to her. Close your eyes and feel her presence within you. Don't try to *do* anything. Just quiet your mind until you sense her Spirit next to your own."

Kaiti closed her eyes, but immediately reopened one, looking quizzically at the Shaman.

Denabi, who was watching her intently, spoke into her mind. *Don't worry, Kitten. It may happen during this moon, or it may take several attempts over the course of the full winter moon. This isn't a test of your abilities. You don't pass or fail. We simply practice together until our efforts are rewarded and our goal is accomplished.*

Not really sure what she was supposed to do, Kaiti slowly closed her eyes again and tried to clear her mind. All she managed was to open herself up to every stray thought or worry she'd had over the last several weeks. Her worries during her mother's recuperation resurfaced, as well as her fear of the king, and the incident with that man who grabbed her in the tent and twisted her arm.

Her nose itched, and when she scratched it, the itch moved to just above her right eye. She shifted her hand up, then realized her right leg was going to sleep. She eased over to the side and pulled her leg out from under her. She straightened it. That made her other leg uncomfortable and she straightened that one as well. She felt Taklishim's hand on her knee and opened her eyes.

He smiled with understanding. "Let's try focusing on the flames instead."

Kaiti saw the fire reflected in the cloudy film covering his eyes. She switched her focus to the flames and listened to his quiet voice.

"Look at the colors. Watch as the yellow meets the orange and then surrounds it. See the tiny flames as they jump away from the larger ones and watch the colors as they blend together..."

Kaiti followed his words as he led her from one image to another. She watched the flames dancing and swirling. There had been many nights after the Shona had retreated into their tents that she'd sat and stared into the fire. She knew the flames, loved the warmth they provided and...

Hello, Kitten. I'm here. Don't look for me. I'm not speaking to you from the physical world. See me in the flames and follow me into the smoke. Follow me, Kitten.

Kaiti saw something moving among the flames, a dark shadow that she thought might be Denabi. She followed and felt a light pull beckoning her into the swirling colors.

The shadow stopped as though waiting for her.

She hurried toward it, not wanting to keep her friend waiting. As she neared the pitch-black mist, the pull became stronger. Pain shot up her spine and she jerked her mental body back and away from the shadow and shrieked in pain. "Stop Denabi! You're hurting me!"

The blackness clawed at her hair, dragging her forward into the flames. A searing pain sliced through her head, sending her reeling toward the edges of the swirling inferno. Her scream echoed through the pathways. Over the sound of her own terrified shriek, Kaiti heard Denabi roar an ear shattering death challenge.

In her mind's eye, she saw Garan leap into the pathways.

Ebi appeared and began tearing at the shadows with her teeth.

Without knowing how she got there, Kaiti suddenly found herself floating near the top of the tent. Looking down, she saw herself lying on the ground with Taklishim's body covering hers.

She watched as Becca ripped open the flap, saw what was happening, and grabbed a nearby bucket of water. The healer threw the entire contents over Kaiti and Taklishim. The icy cold made Kaiti gasp and she felt herself flying back into her chest. The Shaman moaned as Becca gently roll him off her.

In that same instant, a crush of Spirit Guides filled the tent. They surrounded her, facing outward, teeth bared, and hackles raised.

Bree, who'd obviously been running full out, slid into the tent feet first. She tried to get to Kaiti, but a Fisher barred her way with snapping teeth and a high-pitched snarl that no one in their right mind would dare challenge.

Bree feinted to the left, then sidestepped the Guide and shoved him into the canvas wall. She rushed to Kaiti's side.

The Fisher gathered himself to attack, but before he could pounce and tear out Bree's throat, Liris jumped through the opening and tackled him.

Terrified, Kaiti buried her head in Bree's chest.

Completely at a loss as to where the danger might be, Bree pulled Kaiti in close. She wrapped one arm around her, readying a knife in her free hand should it become necessary to defend her cub.

ENOUGH! Denabi's roar preceded her appearance by a millisecond. Everyone froze until she materialized, slightly bloody and battered, with hackles raised and sparks flying from her eyes. Breathing heavily, she spoke with a guttural snarl. *It's over. You all have my thanks for arriving so swiftly. Now please leave us. I'll meet with each of you later to explain.*

Kaiti watched as a Red Fox she didn't recognize, a Mountain Lion and Conn, a Black Ferret she knew from the battle in the glade, slowly relaxed their stance. Each one nodded to Denabi and then faded into the other Realms. She glanced over at Liris, whose Fisher glared malevolently at Bree.

Liris let go of the death grip she had around the Fisher's neck, shrugging an apology to Bree for the actions of her Guide. "You might want to apologize to Legan, Your Grace. He's a fierce protector and would be a good ally for both you and your daughter."

Suddenly feeling weak, Bree closed her eyes and drew in a long, slow breath. When she opened them again, she looked directly at the

Fisher. "I am sorry, Legan, honestly. I didn't know what was happening, and who was friend or foe. All I saw was Kaiti, and you were standing between me and her."

The Fisher gradually relaxed in Liris' arms. *Apology accepted, Duchess. But know this. I will always be on the side of the Spirit Child. If you see me again in a similar situation, know that we are allies, not enemies.* He gradually faded from sight, and Liris quietly got up to leave.

Becca, who was folding Taklishim into a warm, dry blanket, called out to her. "Liris, please go and ask someone to show you to my tent. My bag of herbs is to the right of the opening. I need that, and some more water."

Taklishim lay very still, his skin the color of cold ashes.

Tisneé ducked into the tent just as Liris left. When he saw his chief, his face paled. "Tisneé, go with Liris and show her where my tent is. I sent her for my bag of herbs. Let her bring them to me while you get a bucket of water." She turned to her friend. "Bree, this tent is a muddy mess now. Please find one of your men and have them set up a new tent for Taklishim and get a fire going inside."

Bree nodded and pulled Kaiti up with her. Not sure why she was feeling so weak, she had to lean on the child to keep her balance. "I'll do it on the way to get Kaiti into some dry clothes. I don't know what just happened, but I want some answers when we get everything sorted."

Garan materialized and limped over to Denabi. *It's Ebi, Dens. She's hurt badly. She needs a healer.*

Becca overheard and asked, "Can you get her to the new tent they're going to set up for Taklishim? I can work on her at the same time I help him."

No, I can't carry her.

Garan's worried look frightened Kaiti. If Ebi died because of wounds taken from the Teivaiedin, her mother would die as well. "I'll go. I'll go bring her back."

Bree pulled her to her side. "Oh, no you won't. If there's any way I can go, I will, but you're staying right here in this Realm for now."

Taklishim mumbled something, and Becca leaned closer to hear him better. "Tisneé will go. He...walks the pathways. Not... well, but enough."

When Tisneé returned, Becca told him what needed to happen. If he looked pale already, her words made the color of his skin rival Taklishim's. Pulling his lips into a thin line, he followed Garan out of the tent, apparently going to get Azeel to help him retrieve Ebi.

Bree started toward the door with Kaiti, but Denabi stopped her. *Wait, Duchess.* She padded over to Kaiti and sat down in front of her. *Tell me exactly what just happened, Kitten. It's important.*

Kaiti looked down while trying to collect her thoughts. Her heart still pounded against her ribs and she tried to slow her breathing so she could answer. "I heard you calling me. You said to hear you and follow you into the smoke."

Denabi nodded. *Yes, that was me.*

There was so much more to tell, Kaiti didn't know where to begin. She glanced over at Becca, who held Taklishim cradled on her lap. "I saw a shadow and thought it was you. The shadow waited for me, and I started running to catch up because I didn't want to keep you waiting. Then, you started pulling at me and it hurt and..."

That wasn't me, Kitten. The Teivaiedin must have been waiting for you. I think Taklishim realized what was happening and pulled your consciousness back by physically throwing you to the floor. When you said I was hurting you, I knew immediately what had happened and I called in reinforcements.

The Panther stopped speaking, and with a far-off look in her eye, began listening to something no one else could hear. *I have to go help Ebi, now, Kitten. You go get warm and we'll talk about what happened later.* With that, Denabi was gone.

Bree looked down at the little girl who meant so much to her and to the rest of Anacafria. She realized it was up to her to protect Kaiti here in the physical world, but she was going to have to trust Denabi and the other Guides to protect her from the Teivaiedin.

"Bree, I really need that tent set up. Taklishim used too much of what little energy he has protecting Kaiti."

Bree snapped out of her reverie and moved toward the opening with Kaiti in tow. "We're on our way. I'll be back to help you move him when the tent is ready." Another wave of dizziness overcame her, and she grabbed the tent pole to steady herself. "I think." Using the pole to steady herself, she stepped out into the night.

She looked around for someone she could trust to get the right size tent set up quickly. To her relief, she saw Kalsik making his way to the cook tent for his evening meal. "Kalsik, a moment, please."

Kalsik strode over. It only took a moment for him to see Kaiti's wet clothes and Bree's pale complexion. The cold hung in the air, making it possible to see Kaiti's breath as she stood waiting next to the duchess. He quickly removed his cloak and wound it around the child's shoulders before bowing slightly to Bree. "Your Grace?"

"We had some problems in Taklishim's tent. I need you to find a large replacement tent and get it set up immediately. Conscript as many people as it takes, use my name to get it done as soon as possible. When you're finished, come get me in my tent."

"Immediately, Your Grace." He turned on his heel and hurried toward the supply wagon, grabbing men and women along the way.

Bree ushered Kaiti to their tent, wanting to get her dry and warm before anything else happened that might delay them.

Liris passed them on her way to take Becca her medicine bag. Her eyes held a serious glint Bree hadn't seen before and it gave her a sense of relief to know the woman understood the gravity of the situation.

When Bree and Kaiti arrived at their tent, Kaiti ducked in first. The fright, plus the water Becca had poured on her were making her shiver uncontrollably. Bree brought her dry clothes and she dropped Kalsik's cloak, stripped out of her wet trews and tunic and pulled on the new ones, along with her warm, lambskin coat. The warmth of her dry clothing drove the cold from her bones as she picked up the soaked items and hung them over a line.

Bree watched her, wishing she knew enough Shona to be able to talk to her and ask what happened. She'd heard Denabi ask her questions, but she could neither understand what was asked nor understand Kaiti's answers.

Ebi also concerned her. Her Spirit Guide may be surly and irritable most of the time, but Bree had found over the last few weeks that she'd grown accustomed to having her pop in at the most unexpected times. Usually, the advice the Badger gave was spot on, and, if she was truthful with herself, it was almost always a point of view she hadn't yet considered.

When Kaiti picked up Kalsik's cloak, she looked to her mother, who beckoned for her to follow her outside. When they emerged into the cold night air the increased noise and bustle at the far side of camp made it fairly easy to locate where they were erecting the new tent.

Kalsik had corralled at least ten people, including Darius, to help set up a tent nearly as big as the king's pavilion. Where they'd gotten it, she could only imagine. Judging by the various colored stripes sewn into the sleeves on the helper's tunics, he'd managed to pull in people from just about every region of the kingdom to lend a hand.

As they approached, Bree caught a glimpse of the king on the far side of the tent, hauling on a guide rope he'd thrown over one of the gnarled branches of a nearby tree. Leopold's presence explained why a young archer from Merimeadow worked side-by-side with a grizzled veteran out of Marblefort Downs. The king understood the necessity of building a cohesive fighting unit, and the best way to do that was to have men and women begin to intermingle and work together on every day, mundane projects.

A burly mountain man with a bristling, overflowing beard and an unkempt thatch of bright red hair lifted Darius skyward with a single hand clasping the back of the boy's jade jerkin.

Darius held the other end of the king's rope and was determined to throw it over the branch of a white-barked Finegold tree, so that once they stretched the rope taut, it would form the main support line for the tent.

The giant's grin stretched wide, yellow teeth flashing out of a deeply cragged and sunburned face.

By the looks of him, Bree knew he was one of the mountain people who lived in the northern part of Danforth, in the higher elevations of the Rittendon Peaks. His was a distinctive looking people, generally huge, red-headed, and for the most part easy-going unless someone insulted their kin, their king, or their duchess. People referred to them as Chites because they harvested the extremely rare and valuable azure Alachite gemstones from the mines her great-great-grandfather had opened during the reign of King Sommer II.

To this day, the Duchy of Danforth continued to grow absurdly wealthy from those mines. The Alachite gemstones also explained her family's heraldic colors, which were the crisp, clear blue of an unclouded sky, and the deep, rich gold coveted by kings the world over.

Nordin, Darius' bodyguard, stood by watching the thickly wooded forest, which surrounded the sprawling meadow where they'd made camp. Occasionally he glanced over his shoulder at the prince.

Bree noticed the Chite wink at the burly guard and was surprised when the normally taciturn man grinned back. She wondered if they were life partners—a fairly common occurrence in the king's armies.

She silently approved when Kaiti ran over and returned the cloak to Kalsik. The little girl lowered her eyes when he thanked her, then grabbed a mallet and began pounding in stakes to secure the lower portion of the tent.

Since they were close to completing their task, Bree ducked inside Taklishim's tent where she found Liris holding a steaming cup to the Shaman's lips while Becca held him securely in her arms.

Bree knelt close to Becca's knees. "How is he?"

At the sound of her voice, Taklishim opened his eyes.

Relief washed over her when she saw his amused, sparkling eyes shining out at her.

"I will live, although I am now a much wiser, more cautious teacher than I was a short time ago."

Bree needed to speak with him about Kaiti, but first, she had something else on her mind. "Do you know what's happening with Ebi?"

His eyebrows drew together. "We know she lives, or you would not be kneeling here in my mud." He sent a mock glare at Becca, who looked slightly chagrined.

Sheepishly, the healer shrugged an apology. "Garan said the Teivaiedin were trying to steal Kaiti while she walked the pathways. The only way I could think of to shock her back into her body was to douse her with a bucket full of cold water. Unfortunately, that meant dousing you as well."

It slowly dawned on Bree what Taklishim meant. "What do you

mean I wouldn't be kneeling here?" Her face paled as the implications of Ebi's battle struck her. "If Ebi dies, then I die?"

"What?" Startled, Liris spilled tea onto Taklishim's blanket. She grabbed a dry towel and began mopping distractedly. "What do you mean if she dies, you die? I've never heard of such a thing. Well, actually, I never knew any other Spirit Guides besides Legan, and he never told me anything about that."

Becca took the towel from her. "It's something we discovered during the Battle of the Seven Realms. Somehow Morgrad has freed the Teivaiedin, whom the gods supposedly bound with eternal bonds after the Peshár Wars." She took a closer look at Bree. "And it explains why you look so pale all of a sudden. If Ebi weakens, so do you."

Liris shook her head, obviously confused. "What are the Teivaiedin and what was the Battle of the Seven Realms?"

The tent became crowded as both Garan and the Fisher materialized next to the fire. Garan licked Taklishim's cheek with a quick touch of his tongue. *The tent's ready now. Tisneé, Denabi, and Azeel already have Ebi there. She's regained consciousness and insists she's not hurt as badly as she looks, even though her hide's torn wide open in several places. I swear she's as stubborn as the duchess.* He gave Bree an irritated look before turning and limping out of the tent.

As soon as he left, Tisneé stepped through the opening. He knelt beside Becca and held out his hands to the Shaman, offering to help pull him to his feet. "I'll help you to the tent now, Honored Father."

Bree, who'd stepped back to make room, started forward again despite the dizzying fatigue threatening to overtake her. "Help him? You mean carry him, right? You look worn out from getting Ebi. I'll carry him if you don't have the strength right now."

Tisneé and Becca both turned several shades of red and Taklishim chuckled at their reaction. He spoke while he shifted up onto his knees, using Becca's shoulders to balance himself. "Sometimes, both the Guide and the apprentice lack certain traits. The Badger and the duchess both lack the ability to hear subtleties, yet they make up for this fault by owning hearts only Aevala could make so perfect." He moved his hand to Becca's arm. "Don't worry, White Wolf. Insults are only insulting if intended."

"Insults?" Bree didn't understand. "How is offering to carry someone who's just been through a harrowing physical experience insulting?"

Again, Taklishim smiled. "With the Shona, only infants are carried. From the time a child takes their first step, to the moment he flies on his final journey with the goddess, he should never be carried again. To do otherwise is to imply an absence of worth."

"But your grandson was carrying you the first time I met you."

"He pulled me on a litter." He shrugged. "Perfectly acceptable." With that, Taklishim took Tisneé's outstretched hand, and with Becca's help, got slowly to his feet. The healer placed one of his arms around her shoulder and the warrior did the same with the other. Together, the three of them made their way out of the tent and over to the new, drier accommodations.

When Bree looked at Liris, the woman's wry grin surprised her. Pushing past her on the way to check on Ebi, Bree growled, "I don't find it amusing."

A bark of laughter followed her out of the tent.

Smiling slightly, Bree was mildly surprised by the enjoyable sensations running up her spine at the sound of Liris' laughter. Deliberately pushing those feelings aside, she followed Taklishim to his new tent, where Leopold waited at the entrance holding the flap open for the three of them to enter.

When Bree stepped in behind the others, he stopped her with a hand on her arm and leaned in to whisper in her ear. "I'd love to know why your healer doused my honored guest with a bucket of cold water, and why that warrior," He indicated Tisneé with a lift of his chin, "brought an enormous, bloody Badger into the tent we just set up for Taklishim. Care to enlighten me?"

"As soon as I know, you'll know. The enormous, bloody Badger, as you call her, is my Spirit Guide." She held up a hand when he started to speak. "I have no clue why you can see her right now, all I know is that sometimes I can see Becca's Guide, Garan, and sometimes not, and believe me, I far prefer the latter to the former."

Enormous? You can tell your king he'd better mean strong and powerful rather than slightly plump or he'll be feeling some enormous teeth in his royal backside.

Relieved that she was cranky enough to complain, Bree knelt beside the Badger and examined her wounds.

So, you're not only the high and mighty duchess, you're a healer now?

Bree smiled down at her Guide. "I see you're just as cantankerous as ever. So, the king can see you, can he hear you as well?"

No, he can't, and neither can any of the others, well except for Taklishim, Becca and Kaiti. There's a reason your kind are called the Deaf Ones you know. Not a single brain cell among you. How I ever taught you to see and hear me is anyone's guess and why I got stuck with you, I'll never know.

Denabi, who'd been sitting off to the side licking her own wounds, stopped to listen. *She gets testier than usual when she's hurt. Something I've heard the two of you have in common.*

When Leopold squatted beside Bree, he followed her gaze to where Denabi sat. "Why do you keep looking over there? I don't see anything."

Letting out a deep breath, Bree rubbed tired eyes knowing there was no way she could explain what was happening. "Leo, I honestly don't know all the answers to your questions. I think if you spend some time talking to Taklishim about Spirit Guides instead of tactics, you might get an education worthy of the highest degree possible at the King's Collegium."

Becca settled Taklishim in a warm fur-lined blanket, then went to check on Ebi's injuries. The Badger had several areas where the skin was peeled back from the muscle underneath. The healer glanced around and realized she'd forgotten her medicine bag and water pot back in the other tent.

Bree and the king stood off to the side, talking.

Tisneé had gone to his pallet to rest. Only a very few people walked the Pathways between Realms. When the gift wasn't particularly strong, as in Tisneé's case, the walker usually came back utterly depleted from the experience.

Pushing to her feet, Becca headed for the entrance. Just as she reached out to push aside the flap, Liris stepped in, followed closely by Kaiti, who offered the medicine bag she was holding to Becca. In one hand, Liris held the folding tripod needed to hang the water pot over the fire. In the other, she carried the heavy cauldron filled with water.

Kaiti pointed to the cauldron. "She was going to throw out the water to make it easier to carry, but I made her bring it like it was because I saw how many herbs you put into the pot."

The fur-lined bag Kaiti held was stuffed full of herbs Becca had brought with her from Bodaway's camp. Thinking about the Shona made her homesick for her lover, Nashotah. She'd asked her to come along while she helped Taklishim find the king, but Nashotah insisted she was needed in the camp since they were coming into the time of the winter fever. No one else knew as much about healing that particular sickness as she did. A long sigh escaped her as she took the bag and stepped to where Ebi lay next to the fire.

Liris finished setting up the tripod and hung the heavy pot over the flames. Being somewhat of a perfectionist, she grunted with satisfaction when she had the cauldron hanging at just the right height over the flames. "There." She checked the tripod one final time before glancing over her shoulder at Becca. "I'd be happy to help with the Badger. I'm not sure why I can see her, but I learned some healing from the legion's surgeons. I'm always trying to improve my skills."

"I don't know why you and the king can see her, either." Becca glanced at the shaman, who'd nestled his head deep into the folds of his sleeping furs. "We can ask Taklishim when he wakes up. Anyway, I could use your help. In fact," She glanced at Bree. "Would you mind helping also? If the herbs I use to numb her don't work, I may need someone to hold her down."

"I intended to help anyway. She may be an irascible old hellcat, but I'm getting used to having her around." Bree expected a sharp retort from the Badger, and when she didn't get one, she knelt and stroked the furry head. Ebi's eyes were closed and every so often she'd let out a groan. Bree looked up at Becca. "Do you have something for the pain?"

The king, who was looking more and more perplexed by the minute, took his leave while Liris knelt beside Bree and examined the Badger's gaping wounds.

Becca placed the red medicine bag in her lap and began rummaging through it.

Kaiti brought over a piece of animal hide and laid it out on the ground next to the healer's feet. She pointed to the bag. "It'd be easier if you put them out on the furs. I'll set them up the way Adené taught me." Adené, the healer in Dahana's camp, often included Kaiti whenever his skills were needed to heal the animals kept by the tribe.

Distracted by the severity of Ebi's wounds, Becca simply nodded. "Thanks." Dumping the contents of her bag onto the pelt, she sorted through them until she found the herb she needed to staunch the bleeding. She made a swirling motion with her finger over the rest of the bags. "Would you look through all of these and find the green pouch?"

She looked around for a cup, but since they'd just erected the tent, no one had brought in any supplies "Tane's blood. It's hard enough working out of a saddle bag, let alone someone else's living quarters."

She glanced up at Liris. "Would you go back to my tent and look in my left saddlebag? It should be propped up next to the door. There's a funnel and a wooden cup I use to get my herbal teas down someone's throat when they're unconscious."

As Liris nodded and hurried out, Becca called after her. "And find Kalsik and tell him I need some of the cloth he brought along to polish his swords. Make sure it's clean though."

Liris stuck her head back into the tent. "Kalsik's the bodyguard and weapon's master for the prince?"

"Right."

"On my way." Liris made sure the flap closed after she left. She wove her way through a maze of tents and campfires. The numbers of soldiers and camp personnel had steadily increased in the short couple of days she'd been riding with the Anacafrians.

The order Jathez imposed upon the camp impressed her. He'd set strict rules about the placement of latrines, and she'd watched as he'd inspected each one himself to make sure his commanders followed his orders to a tee. No Estian lord commander would stoop to such menial tasks, but then, Liris had been in encampments where disease had run rampant through the troops. Jathez also gave each company a designated location to pitch their tents. He'd had Cameron meticulously organize the travel kitchens, placing them at specific intervals around the camp, and he made sure each soldier had a designated cook fire where they were to get their daily meals.

When she passed Bree's tent, her mind wandered to the duchess. The handsome woman had caught her attention the moment she'd come to stand in front of the king. Unlike Estia, noble born Anacafrian women didn't serve in the armies, yet here was a duchess, a cousin to the king, who not only wore throwing knives strapped across her chest, but who actually commanded half of the king's army. Her attractions usually ran to strong women, and she felt a familiar stirring in her belly that had nothing to do with the fact that she'd missed her dinner.

Legan appeared by her side. He jogged next to her on the way to Becca's tent. *You're not a noble anymore, Lir. She's about as far out of your league now as that peasant woman was back in Corin.*

"Ah, but that peasant woman, as you call her, enjoyed my company as much as I enjoyed hers. We just had to be a little more discreet about our activities, that's all. And, simply because I have this cursed brand on my cheek doesn't mean I don't still have noble blood running through my veins. I may be lower than that cook boy over there as far as rank goes around here, but blood tells." She grinned down at him. "And you know how I get when my blood starts telling."

Yes, I'm well aware of your proclivities. Garan says she's still grieving the loss of her wife. What happens if she never wants to get into a relationship again?

They came to Becca's tent, which was three away from where Bree had positioned hers. She had just begun untying the laces holding the flap closed when a man approached. "Here now, that's not your tent. When you're in the king's service, rules apply. If a tent's tied closed, nobody goes in."

Legan disappeared as Liris turned to face the man.

When she did, his eyes widened. "You're the one from Estia." He hesitated a moment before stepping over and offering his arm in the typical greeting of soldiers—forearm to forearm.

Liris glanced down at the proffered arm. If she took it and he had any hostile intentions, she'd be in a very bad fighting position. The man stood about a head taller than she did, burly in a refined sort of way. She decided to chance it and grasped his forearm.

"My name's Kon. I'm one of the sub-commanders from Thadon. One of your people, Leez, has been helping me fletch arrows at night. He told me why you got that mark, and I have to tell you, if I'd have been there that day, I'd have one on my cheek as well."

Smiling, Liris retrieved her arm. "I'm Liris, and there aren't any better fletchers around than Leez. His father maintained the weapons for his garrison. Leez has been cleaning swords and making arrows since he was about five."

She turned and pointed at the bindings on Becca's tent. "Becca asked me to bring her something from her tent, that's why I was going inside. Nothing more sinister than that."

A scuffle taking place at one of the cook tents momentarily distracted Kon and a low growl erupted from deep within his chest. "I have to go knock some heads together. I'm glad I finally met you." He turned and strode toward the two combatants.

Liris watched him grab each man by the back of their tunics to separate them. She couldn't remember how many times she'd done the exact same thing to various members of her troops in Estia, once again marveling at the similarities of command no matter what kingdom you served.

After retrieving the funnel and cup from the saddlebags, she quickly walked through the camp trying to find Kalsik. Time was of the essence, but it wasn't easy locating one person among four hundred or more soldiers.

The sounds of the camp as she searched were a comfort. She'd been in military service since her parents had given her to Sir Randaf as a seven-year-old page. An undercurrent of voices always echoed throughout a camp, and here was no exception. Murmurs, laughter and the occasional argument floated on the air, accompanied by the sounds of stone on metal as people sharpened their weapons.

The clacking of wooden practice swords caught her ear and she headed that way hoping Kalsik was nearby.

Legan reappeared next to her leg. *Garan said that Becca needs those supplies quickly. I told him you're hurrying and that you're trying to find Kalsik. He's over where they're practicing swordplay.*

"I see him. Would you tell Garan I'll be there as quickly as I can?"

Legan disappeared, and Liris walked over to where Kalsik sorted through a stack of practice swords. "You're Kalsik?"

The man turned and nodded. "I am."

"Becca, the healer who came with Taklishim, needs some of the extra cloth you brought with you. They're for washing out some wounds, so they need to be clean."

Sighing, the young man reluctantly slid the practice sword back into the barrel. "I was hoping for a mere five minutes to practice on my own tonight, but as usual," He gave a playful bow, "My services are indispensable."

Liris returned his half smile and followed him to his tent where he produced several new pieces of cloth from a carry sack. She sorted through the neatly folded items, taking those she thought were the right size and material for the job. "Are these okay?"

"They're yours."

"Thanks!" Running across the encampment, she ducked under and around flickering lanterns that were strategically placed to illuminate the footpaths. Mist had settled over the camp, and she followed the yellow haze of lights to Taklishim's tent where she hurried in and handed Becca the pieces of cloth. "How is she?"

The healer's jaw rippled as she took the material. "Not good. Look at this blackening of her skin here." She pulled up a flap of hide, then pointed to another. "And here. I've never seen infection set in so quickly. I hope we're not seeing another advantage for the Teivaiedin, where their bites fester more rapidly than we can control the contagion."

Kaiti sat quietly in a corner watching. She hadn't yet seen the blackness on Ebi's skin, but when Becca pointed to it, she quickly scooted over. "Adené stopped the blackness on one of Bodaway's horses once after a boar tore through the muscle in his leg. The boar had some type of poison on his tusks, and the gash became that color after a few days. He used a special moss."

When the herbal tea heating over the fire began to steam, Becca poured some into a small cup, which she handed to Liris. "Here, take this outside and stand with it until it cools. If there's any snow or cold water around, put the cup into it. When it's cool, bring it back in."

Once Liris had left, Becca put one of the rags into a second pot of water heating directly in the coals of the fire. "Did he use the powder from a purple fungus?"

"No. He tried that first, but it didn't work." Kaiti anxiously sorted through all the medicine pouches, opening each one and peering inside. She sniffed several but didn't find what she was looking for. "It's not here." She stood and started for the door.

After what had happened with the Teivaiedin, Bree felt uneasy letting her out of her sight. "Kaiti, where are you going?"

Kaiti heard her name and turned toward her mother, then to Becca for a translation. Once she understood the question, she answered quickly. "I know what the plant looks like. Adené took me with him to hunt for it. I have to go find some."

Becca translated for Bree who glanced down at Ebi, then back to Kaiti.

Bree stroked Ebi's fur, scratching just behind the ears where her dogs loved to be stroked. Becca needed her help, and she was feeling weaker by the minute, but she also knew she wasn't going to allow Kaiti to go off on her own to find the plant in the middle of the forest. She chided herself for having such an irrational fear. The child had basically raised herself in the forests where the nomadic Shona lived and was well able to care for herself. But still...

Liris came back with the cooled herb tea and handed it to Becca.

Sitting back on her haunches, Bree studied the Estian. She watched her kneel next to Becca, who handed her the wet cloth she'd been using to clean the wounds. Bree touched the healer's hand. "Wait Becs." She took the cloth from Liris who looked up with lowered brows. "I need a favor from you. We hardly know each other, but I know you're a warrior who can take care of herself. My daughter," She nodded toward the child standing by the tent opening, "Kaiti, needs to go into the forest to find some kind of plant that will stop the spread of this black infection. It's dark out, and although she knows the forest better than anyone here in camp, I—"

Liris held up her hand. "Say no more, Duchess. I'll take her with me to get my shortsword and go out with her."

Bree hesitated. She hadn't really thought out her request and the idea of sending Kaiti out into the darkness with someone she'd only met briefly a few days earlier sounded only nominally better than sending her out alone.

Liris picked up on Bree's hesitation. "I'll defend her with my life, Your Grace. In fact, one of my men, Leez, considers the forest his home and he's deadly with a bow. I'll take him with us as well."

Nodding, Bree dunked the rag into the pot and wrung it out. "Thank you. She's pretty stubborn, but she knows what she's looking for. Becs, would you let her know... Liris is it?"

Liris nodded.

"Tell her Liris is going with her."

Being completely absorbed by the severity of Ebi's wounds, Becca hadn't been paying attention to the conversation. "What?"

"Would you let Kaiti know that Liris is going with her to look for that plant?"

Liris stared at Kaiti. "She doesn't speak Anacafrian?"

"It's a long story."

Becca translated while she measured some more herbs into the cold tea.

Once Kaiti understood that she'd be allowed to go, she didn't wait for Liris. She leapt out of the tent heading for the surrounding forest.

Liris ran after her and grabbed an arm. "Whoa, whoa. Hold up. I need to get my weapons." She mimed stabbing someone and slashed her fist through the air a few times. "My weapons."

Kaiti sighed and rolled her eyes. They didn't have time to wait, but she followed the scarred woman to her tent and waited while she armed herself. The woman called out to a man sitting with several soldiers around a campfire.

The man answered, then went to another tent and retrieved a bow and a quiver full of arrows. When he joined them, Kaiti saw that he had an identical scar burned into his cheek, the same curved line the woman had. She shifted impatiently from one foot to another, anxiously waiting while the woman spoke to the man. Although the delay hadn't been very long, she grew more and more restless with each passing moment.

Finally, Liris motioned for her to lead them out to the forest. Once among the trees, Kaiti felt at home again. The land under the canopy of branches sang a familiar song as she walked quietly through the carpet of fallen leaves. The songs of crickets, owls, and nighthawks mesmerized her so that she completely forgot about the two warriors who accompanied her.

Putting aside the night sounds, she concentrated on locating the moss—a rare species and difficult to find. Adené had said it only grew in the crook of a Finegold tree, and only if the tree grew near a certain kind of bush that blossoms with red flowers and yellow berries. The name of the plant eluded her, but she crisscrossed the forest, automatically dodging spiny thorns and skirting around poisonous deathtail leaves. It took an entire candlemark before she found a bush with the yellow berries. Turning in a circle, she scanned the area hoping to see a towering Finegold tree.

To her surprise, neither the woman, nor the man, was with her anymore. She quickly squatted beneath an elephant leaf, her gaze darting back and forth trying to locate her companions. The forest could be dangerous at night and she would have been taking more precautions if she'd known they weren't nearby to protect her while she concentrated on finding the moss.

She looked up and to the right, then visually tracked backward when she realized a shadow on a branch about twenty feet above the forest floor hadn't quite fit with what she'd expected to see. She moved her gaze slowly over the same branch, hoping to find what her subconscious had registered the first time she'd searched. When she found it again, she breathed a sigh of relief. What she'd seen was a dark silhouette using the tree's massive trunk as camouflage. The man's clothes blended so perfectly with the brown pitting of the thick bark that it made it nearly impossible to see him.

She turned her attention to the surrounding forest, looking for the woman, who waved at her from not more than ten paces away. The movement startled her, and she took an involuntary step back. Very few people could come that close without Kaiti sensing their presence. These two seemed more comfortable moving through the forest than even the best of the Shona trackers.

Reassured, Kaiti rose and took off through the forest again. There hadn't been a Finegold tree near the bush she'd found, so once again she moved with the natural grace of a panther, silent but sure of her every move. Every now and again, she'd glance up into the trees to follow the dark figure as he gracefully leapt between branches, his soft-soled boots settling onto limbs with flawless precision, his weight distributed precisely so as not to move a single leaf or cause even the slightest bit of sound.

She neither saw nor heard the woman again, but after seeing her skills, she trusted that she remained close by. Tiny sparks of doubt crept over her when, after what seemed like several candlemarks, she hadn't found the right combination of plants. Every Finegold she found lacked the nearby berry bush, and each time she came upon a berry bush, there were none of the majestic Finegolds close enough to harbor the mossy herb.

She'd just pulled herself over yet another a fallen log when she heard a quick whistle from the man in the trees. Immediately crouching low, she warily scanning her surroundings. There didn't appear to be any danger, so she looked up and saw that the man had allowed himself to be silhouetted by the light of the moon. Lifting his arm in an exaggerated motion, he pointed off to her right.

The foggy mist had grown thick, and she moved slowly in the direction he'd indicated, every now and again visually checking in with him to make sure she didn't walk into any danger. After she'd walked several paces, she ducked under a large yew leaf and her heart leapt for joy. Not twenty paces away stood a towering Finegold with a yellow berry bush nestled in close to the tree's white trunk. She turned and raised her fist in triumphant acknowledgement of the man's discovery. Even though darkness surrounded him, the flash of white from his smile told her he was also pleased with the find.

Running to the base of the tree, she grabbed onto the trunk and began shimmying up, using the knots and tiny branches for hand and footholds.

The man leapt to a branch above her. Judging by his concerned expression, he was obviously unsure of her climbing abilities.

Kaiti pointed above him, indicating she only had a short way to go before she reached the moss, whose velvety green hood was just barely visible from their lower vantage point. She continued climbing past him with him following close on her heels.

As she fumbled for handholds in the dark, she began speaking out loud to the tree, just as she'd heard Adené speaking on their journey. "Tree Spirit, I need your help. I need a tiny portion of your gift of healing. In return, if possible, I'll stand guard between you and your enemies."

The branches thinned the closer she came to the juncture where the tree split into two mighty trunks, each one so massive that a grown man would be unable to reach completely around their circumference. Pausing before she pushed to the final branch, she placed her cheek up against the bark and whispered, "Tree Spirit. Please."

Setting her foot firmly against a knot, she grabbed a final limb and pulled herself up until she could peek over the edge of the V where the two trunks came together. There, right where she'd hoped it would be, was the emerald green moss that Adené had used.

She ran her fingers over the velvety top before reaching down and pulling a small bag from an inside pocket of her tunic. When she realized she'd forgotten to bring her knife, she looked down at Leez and pointed to his.

He climbed a little higher, pulled his blade from its sheath and cut off one of the bumps. Very carefully, so as not to accidentally drop it, he scooped the moss onto the blade and lowered it down to her.

Just as carefully, she opened her hand so he could slide the tiny bit of plant onto her palm. A slight breeze rustled through the leaves and she quickly put the moss into her pouch before it could accidentally blow away.

Leez reached up to cut some more, but she put her small hand on top of his. When he met her gaze, she shook her head. "Adené said the Tree Spirit would only give us a little bit. We have all we need."

Leez brought his eyebrows together and shrugged as he put the knife back in its sheath. "Ya don' talk normal, and I don' unnerstan' ya, but Liris said yer the boss."

Kaiti shyly returned his smile, then started down to the forest floor.

CHAPTER 6

The three of them walked into a quiet camp. Most everyone slept, except for the sentries who watched their approach and announced them to the camp with a short, trilling whistle.

Kaiti waived to one of them, making sure he recognized her before she took off running to Taklishim's tent. All was quiet except for the crackling of the fires and the occasional snarl of camp dogs as they roamed the vicinity of the cook tents in search of discarded bones and bread.

As she approached the area where Kalsik had supervised the pitching of Taklishim's new tent, she saw Tisneé kneeling next to a fire, rubbing his hands together over the flames. She slowed her pace, respectfully lowering her eyes as she passed.

His quiet voice startled her. "Good hunting?"

She gave a shy, barely perceptible nod, then brushed aside the flap of the tent and slipped inside.

Becca still sat next to Ebi, whose face seemed to have lost some of its earlier signs of distress. Her mother rested against the log, intently watching the flap. She bolted upright when she saw her enter, relief relaxing the worry lines stretching out from her eyes and mouth.

Kaiti pulled the pouch from beneath her shirt, knelt beside Becca and dumped the green moss onto her hand.

Becca felt the smooth texture of the plant. "Are you sure that's enough? I've never seen this before."

"It's enough. Adené said to never take more than you need because the Tree Spirit needs it too. He said if you take too much and keep it longer than a day, it turns into a poison because you angered the Spirit."

"So, how do I prepare it? Do I put it directly on the blackness?"

"No. Grind it into a powder, then put it in honey."

"Honey?" Becca's eyes narrowed. "Well, Adené's never been the cleverest of men, but he has an uncanny ability to see a healing plant and know exactly what to do with it. His grandmother had the same gift. Here," Becca picked up two fairly good-sized rocks; one oval and flat and one oblong with two rounded ends. "I thought you might need these to grind it up."

When Liris joined them, Bree glanced up and nodded her thanks.

Liris dipped her head in response.

Becca ran a tired hand through her hair and addressed the Estian. "I'm sorry to be using you as an errand girl, Liris, but I need one more favor."

Liris shrugged. "I don't sleep much anyway. What do you need?"

Becca pointed to the moss. "Kaiti says we need to mix this with honey and obviously I don't have any here right now."

"I'll go find a cook and get some for you."

Bree got stiffly to her feet. "I'll go with you. Ebi's resting quietly now that Becca's dosed her with that awful concoction of hers. I had two weeks of her pouring that stuff down my throat. It works, but it tastes deadly." They stepped outside as Kaiti took the oblong stone and began grinding the moss into a fine powder.

Bree stopped a moment and stretched aching arms before following Liris to her cook's tent. She'd begun to think of the irascible woman as "her cook" ever since she'd told Cameron to add her to the battalion rosters.

The cooking areas stood out from the other parts of the encampment because they were generally surrounded by the wagons used to haul the pots, pans, utensils and food. By this time of night, the cook's apprentices had hung all of the ladles and pans on lines strung between nearby trees. Bree and Liris ducked under one of them to get to where the cook watched a young woman bank the fire. Bree's shoulder bumped the handle of a hanging pot, which in turn clanged loudly against its neighbor.

Not particular about whom she shared her ire with, the cook glared at Bree while automatically reaching out to steady the cookware. When the pots quieted to her satisfaction, she slowly wiped her hands on her apron. "Ah heerd there was mair trooble wi' th' bairn. Is she aw reit?"

"She's fine. Thank you for asking." Bree motioned with her chin. "This is Liris. Liris, this is..." Bree blinked as she realized she'd never asked the woman her name.

Luckily, the woman didn't hesitate. She squinted at the scar on Liris' cheek. "Yoo're th' hen wi' th' honur. Yoo're welcome at mah table enytime. Aam Kirin."

Liris nodded. "I've heard you keep the best table in the camps. Thank you."

Kirin raised skeptical eyebrows. "Dornt ye hae a quick tongue? Ah'll nae be feedin' ye anymair fur 'at." She brushed some stray flour off her sleeve, then glared up at Bree. "Noo, whit dae ye need, Yer Grace? Mah tent's closed."

"Do you have any honey? Becca needs it for a poultice."

"Ay coorse ah do." She stepped over to the closest wagon and rummaged around for a while. It seemed as though she'd decided to reorganize her entire inventory before she straightened and held out a large jar.

Bree accepted it quickly, not wanting to further irritate the woman.

"Luck be wi' ye 'en." Before Bree could thank her, Kirin turned and headed off to her sleeping tent.

Bree pried loose the cork, stuck her finger in the jar and pulled out some of the golden honey. She slipped her finger into her mouth, closed her eyes and enjoyed the slippery, sweet taste. Sighing, she offered the jar to Liris. "You can taste Danforth in this honey. It's the only duchy where the bees pollinate the Roseberry Bush and produce the finest treat in all of Anacafria. Here, try some."

Liris' eyes sparkled as she bit her lip, the right side of her mouth pulling up into a mischievous grin.

Legan spoke into her mind. *Easy now. You don't know her well enough... although if I didn't know better, I'd say she handed that one to you on a silver platter.*

Liris acknowledged the truth of his words with a sigh and dipped her finger in. She pulled out a large dollop and slowly licked it off. "Mmmmm. I've never tasted anything quite like it before. If this is what Danforth tastes like," She held Bree's gaze a second longer than necessary, "then I'd love to enjoy its sweetness as often as I possibly can."

As Bree watched Liris slowly lick the honey from her finger, she felt a familiar stirring and recognized a longing within herself that she thought she'd never experience again. There'd been times when just the fruity fragrance of a Roseberry Bush would remind her of her wife, of how she would ride miles out of her way to bring her a jar from the bee witch who lived on the upper edge of the Ironmoor forest.

Sadness suddenly overtook her, and her loss overrode any feelings that might have begun to sneak into her shuttered heart. She corked the jar and started for Taklishim's tent. "C'mon. Let's get this back to Becca."

Liris yawned, covering her mouth with the back of her hand. "With your permission, Your Grace, I need to get some sleep."

"Call me Your Grace or Commander in a formal setting, but Bree is fine in private or otherwise. I've never really followed the habits of the nobility."

Liris snorted. "I never liked the game playing, or the backstabbing either. Give me a common born any day to some lordly popinjay in silk tights."

Bree nodded, acknowledging the truth to her words. "Sleep well, then. I'll probably stay here when the king continues on tomorrow. I don't think Ebi will be able to travel. I'll catch up later."

Somewhat disappointed, but not surprised, Liris got her bearings on exactly where she was in relation to her tent and made her way to the warm, welcome comforts of her bedroll.

Bree hurried back to Becca and held out the jar of honey.

Kaiti took it instead and set it carefully on the ground, making sure the area was level enough that it wouldn't tip. She poured a portion into an iron pot, then set it on a large rock Becca had placed in the middle of a low fire. Taking a pinch of the pulverized moss, she mixed it into the honey and stirred with a small stick. She repeated the process several times, each time peering intently into the pot after she'd stirred.

Curious, Becca leaned over to see the ingredients. "What are you looking for?"

Kaiti added another small amount and began stirring again. "Adené said to add a little, then watch for tiny bubbles to start forming. When you see them, it's ready. If you keep adding more powder after you see bubbles, it'll make the wound worse and kill the animal."

The herbal sleeping draught Becca had given Ebi was wearing off. The Badger let out a quiet groan and moved her front paw feebly. The healer picked up the small funnel and dipped her wooden cup into the bowl full of the herbal mixture she'd prepared earlier.

Bree, who'd helped administer two previous doses, stepped around behind Ebi and held her head between her hands.

Becca carefully placed the funnel into the Badger's mouth and administered the drink in small portions, making sure most of it went down Ebi's throat and not onto the fur on her neck, or worse, into her lungs. When she finished, she looked over her shoulder to see if Kaiti's poultice had begun to bubble.

Kaiti sat quietly next to the kettle. When she noticed Becca checking her work, she took a rag and picked up the kettle by its wire handle. She offered it to Becca, who took it and brought it close to the wounded Badger. Kaiti knelt next to Ebi and gave Becca one more set of instructions. "It has to go on pretty hot to kill the blackness."

Curious, the healer studied the potion with a critical eye. Kaiti had been right. Tiny bubbles broke the surface at short intervals. She picked up a large cooking ladle and used the flat end to apply the sticky mixture to Ebi's wounds. The blackness had spread to parts of her body not initially injured during the attack.

Bree was one of her best friends, but more importantly—at least for now anyway—she was an excellent tactician with an uncanny ability to second guess an opposing commander and pull victory out of impending disaster. Great responsibility rested on the duchess' shoulders, and Becca intended to make sure those shoulders were strong and straight and able to carry whatever load she needed to carry. The king needed her, Kaiti needed her, and by extension, the Spirit Guides needed her to provide a safe harbor for the Spirit Child.

As she worked, she glanced up at Bree. Worry lines creased her friend's brow, but Becca knew she was more concerned about Ebi and Kaiti than about the possible consequences to herself should her Spirit Guide die. Becca nodded her reassurance, then pointed to the Badger's neck. "Could you lift that flap of skin there, near her ear?"

Bree carefully peeled back the skin and Becca slathered on the honey. While she worked, Becca thought about her immediate future. She'd planned to return to Dahana's camp shortly after getting Taklishim and Tisneé settled, but now she felt Bree needed her here. Nashotah would understand. They'd been separated for long periods before, but the separations still bothered her. She missed her friend's wisdom, especially the commonsense approach Nashotah took whenever unusual problems presented themselves.

Glancing at Bree again, she set the honey pot down and sat back on her haunches. "I hope this mixture works. Adené has a unique ability to mix herbs with the most unlikely substances. He's worked miracles with patients who would otherwise have died."

Bree sat back as well, settling against the riding pad she'd propped against a log to give her some support. "I've heard you and Nashotah tease Adené about being an impulsive, ill-tempered giant. For some reason, my impression of him has always been that of a huge child, completely devoted to Dahana and Nashotah, but dangerous if provoked."

Kaiti moved over to lie down beside Bree, using part of the saddle pad as a pillow.

Becca watched her a second, thinking about how best to describe

Nashotah's twin. "Do you know what Adené means in the Shona language?" When Bree shook her head, Becca smiled. "When Nashotah and Adené were born, their parents asked Taklishim and his wife, Kayah, to name them. Kayah gave Nashotah her name, which means 'loving protector.' Taklishim named Adené after Adené's Spirit Guide, the Cricket."

Bree chuckled as she thought of the huge Adené having a Cricket as a Guide. "Who chooses the Guides?"

Becca shrugged. "They choose us, I think. Or Aevala assigns them to us. I'm not really clear about how that works. Anyway, a Cricket has a unique ability to adapt. I think that along with teaching Adené to adapt to situations, his Guide, Minet, also teaches him to modify, or adapt, various medicines in unique ways. He has a gift for it, even though the other aspects of the cricket—the tendency to be led by his emotions and be impulsive—are far more common occurrences for the big, lovable brute."

Thinking about Adené and his Cricket, Bree pointed to Ebi. "Well, let's hope he and his Guide are right about this potion. Ebi's too important to the battle with the Teivaiedin. They need all the Guides they can muster right now."

Becca pointed to the sleeping child. "Why don't you two go back to your tent and get some sleep. I'll take the first watch and come wake you when I can't keep my eyes open any longer."

As she watched Bree pick up Kaiti with such loving care, she realized a lot of healing had taken place in her friend's life in the last few months. When they were younger, she'd watched Bree move through a succession of lovers, but she'd never seen her love someone as strongly as she'd loved Timur. She, and others, had worried that Bree might take her own life after Timur died. Now she'd opened herself up to love again, and Becca smiled as she watched her tenderly carry her from the tent.

At the beginning of the second watch, Becca slipped into Bree's tent and woke her before trading places with her on the cot. By silent agreement, neither felt comfortable leaving Kaiti alone in the middle of the night.

Bree walked back to where Taklishim and Ebi lay quietly sleeping.

She picked a flaming stick out of the fire and held it over the Badger to get a better look at her wounds. She couldn't be absolutely certain, but it seemed as though the black hadn't spread any further than when she'd gone to bed.

She moved the flame closer to Taklishim and was surprised to see him watching her through heavy-lidded eyes. She spoke quietly. "I thought you'd sleep through the night. Did I wake you when I came in?"

He shook his head. "No. The Spirit Child not being able to safely walk the pathways troubles me. So," He shrugged. "I use the night to bring possibilities into my mind."

"Will you take her back any time soon?"

Acoma, Taklishim's Guide, strode into the tent and lay down next to the Shaman. *We'll be more on guard, Duchess. They took us by surprise. It won't happen again.*

The Fox and Bree eyed each other. Acoma's wisdom was legendary. In fact, several songs had been sung about him around many campfires. As a child and then as a young woman, she'd believed the minstrels were singing about a mythical creature taken straight out of the Shona legends. Yet here she was staring into his golden eyes.

She glanced away, then looked back. "The last time I saw Garan and Denabi, they'd been injured as well. Are they being treated? Have their injuries turned black like Ebi's?"

They are well, and no, there is no blackness. We think perhaps there were two Teivaiedin waiting along the pathways. Garan and Denabi fought one, and Ebi another. The poison came only from the one Ebi fought.

Bree thought about that a second. "That makes sense. If Garan and Denabi fought say, a lion, there wouldn't be any poison, but if they'd fought an adder, it would be a different outcome all together."

Yellow-gold eyes blinked back at her, acknowledging her insight.

Bree turned to Taklishim. "Can Kaiti actually see what kind of animal our Guides are fighting?"

Taklishim considered her question. "Becca told me that during the battle with my grandson and his followers, Kaiti told the Guides what animal was attacking." The old man glanced at the roof of the tent, thinking. "But, Kaiti said she only saw a dark shadow on the pathways, which she mistook for Denabi."

"So, she can see the animals in this Realm, but not on the pathways?"

Acoma considered the possibility. *That's one conclusion. There are other possibilities as well.*

Bree held up her hand and began counting on her fingers. "One, she can see the animals in this Realm, but not on the pathways, or two, she's never walked the pathways before and may need to spend more time there to acclimate herself to the experience. Three, the Teivaiedin can disguise themselves when they are on the pathways and she needs to learn how to see through their camouflage.

Another question I have is whether they always work in concert with a human. If that's the case, perhaps we should ask the Spirit Child to open her awareness while walking the camp.

"The king will probably move on tomorrow and I plan to keep Kaiti here with me while Ebi heals. When we catch up to the army again, I'll talk to her about it."

Bree lowered herself down until she was resting against the log. She turned to Taklishim. "Do you plan to go with Leopold, or will you stay here until you get your strength back?"

"Tisneé and I will ride with the king." Sometime during the night, while Bree slept, Tisneé had brought all of the Shona's belongings, including their bedrolls, into the tent and had bedded down for the night. Taklishim glanced at his sleeping form, then slowly closed his eyes to rest.

Bree added a few sticks to their fire before closing her eyes as well. She wouldn't sleep. She'd been on too many night patrols to allow herself to nod off. Staying awake while exhausted was second nature, and she knew she'd restore her strength simply by sitting quietly in the dark listening to the sounds of a nighttime bivouac.

Shortly before dawn, as the scent of cinnamon and ginger wafted on the air, Leopold entered. He held the flap aside for Eavan, who followed him inside balancing five bowls of sweetly spiced porridge on a small tray.

Becca, who'd come in a short time earlier, glanced up from

checking on Ebi. The big Badger had regained consciousness as the sun's rays began streaming in through the cracks around the tent flap.

Tisneé rose and accepted two of the bowls, one for himself and the other for his chief.

Eavan handed two bowls to the king and to Becca.

Bree took the third while the king lowered himself onto the log next to her and asked, "How's the Badger doing?"

Ebi weakly lifted her head and glared at the king. *Tell him "the Badger" has a name and he'd do well to use it.*

Chuckling, Bree relayed the message. Leopold's look of incredulity told her he hadn't yet fully accepted the idea of Spirit Guides, let alone irascible ones with sharp tongues.

He stared at Ebi, then decided Spirit Guide or not, he wasn't used to being addressed in such a manor. "Tell "the Badger" that "the king" shall be spoken of as, His Majesty, if she knows what's good for her." He scooped a spoonful of mash into his mouth and met Ebi's glare with one of his own.

Ebi's eyes narrowed and she snapped her teeth in the king's direction. *I'll address you however I want, you...*

Ebi. Acoma sat by Taklishim's side. He lowered his head until his eyes were level with hers. *At the very least, he is Taklishim's friend. Besides, Aevala herself anointed him king, so curb your tongue and save your strength to heal yourself.*

Bree quietly sat back and enjoyed the repartee.

Leopold continued to glare while eating his gruel.

Ebi grumbled but lay back and closed her eyes again.

Taklishim had just opened his mouth to speak when a shrill whistle sounded at the edge of the camp. Each of the perimeter sentries repeated the warning, and both Bree and the king jumped to their feet.

Leopold dropped his bowl in the dirt as he rose, and now rested his hand on the hilt of his sword. Each warning had its own distinct sequence of notes, and he stood rooted in place as he carefully interpreted the message. "Riders, and obviously not more of our soldiers or they wouldn't have raised the alarm. Come on. Let's go see who they are."

As Bree and the king stepped through the opening of the tent, four of Leopold's guards hastily assembled from various locations throughout the camp. Two flanked him and two fell into step behind. He and Bree strode through camp in the direction of the first warning whistle.

Bree automatically took stock of the troops, noticing which of her units were already falling into formation and which were still trying to get organized. She also watched Darius half run, half walk from his tent to join his father. She schooled her amusement into a more serious expression as he approached because it was obvious his excitement was warring with the other day's admonition to be controlled and dignified at all times.

Jathez stalked through the throng of soldiers who were hastily grabbing swords and shields. He fell into step beside the king, replacing the bodyguard on the left who moved a distance away while still maintaining the pace set by the king.

Kaiti elbowed her way between the two trailing guards and handed her mother the bandoliers she customarily wore strapped across her chest. Bree winked at her as she took them, letting Kaiti know things probably weren't as serious as they looked. As they walked, she shrugged into the harness and settled the knives into place.

Kaiti and Darius took their places behind the king's guards and Nordin and Kalsik walked a short distance behind them. When the party crested the hill and approached the sentry, the man quickly brought his fist to his chest.

Jathez acknowledged the salute with a nod. "Report."

The man held up a lean, muscular arm and pointed to the east where a cloud of dust—and the forms of nearly a hundred riders—could be seen silhouetted in the vibrant colors of the breaking dawn. "The way they're riding, I'd say they're Shona, Sir. They're riding straight for us. I estimate about a hundred or more warriors."

The king quickly turned to look down at the picket lines of his cavalry unit. The area around the horses was a beehive of activity.

He urgently grabbed Jathez' arm. "Get to the cavalry. Have them mount up, but no one rides out unless I, or you, or Bree give the command. Go yourself. I want no mistakes, and no hotheaded young officers riding out to make a name for themselves."

Jathez nodded quickly and then hurried down the hill.

After a second glance at the Shona riders, Leopold gestured for Darius and Kaiti to come closer. When they did, he put his arm around Darius' shoulder. "This time, Son, I want you to run as fast as you can to get my horse. Take Kaiti with you and have her saddle your cousin's horse as well. We'll be back at Taklishim's tent. Bring the horses there."

He stopped the boy just as he turned toward the picket line where their horses were tethered. "Remember, haste is fine at times, but don't let anyone think you're worried, or frightened."

Darius came to attention and gave his father a military salute. After his father acknowledged the gesture, the prince grabbed Kaiti's arm, pulling her along at a breakneck speed down the hill and through the camp.

Nordin and Kalsik, holding their swords swiveled at a ninety-degree angle, had to run to keep up as well.

Bree shielded her eyes from the rising sun, trying to see if the warriors wore face paint or if they'd covered their bodies with the white ash they used to frighten their enemies during a battle.

Leopold stepped up beside her. "What do you think?"

"I don't think their faces are painted, and from this distance, they don't look like they're covered in ash. They're riding at a slow, steady pace. My guess is they don't mean to attack."

Eavan ran up the hill and quickly bowed. "I'm sorry it took me so long to get here, Sire. I had to get a medic to some fool who tripped on a tent wire and knocked himself unconscious."

Leopold gave her a withering look. "Next time use your authority as my squire and conscript someone else to get help. When an alarm is sounded, your place is by my side."

Pink suffused the young woman's face, but she straightened her shoulders and answered briskly. "Yes, Sire."

Turning back to watch the riders, he shielded his eyes from the sun. "I think I agree with your assessment, Cousin." He motioned to one of his guards. "Rocca, I want you to go find Marshals Sandresin and Toker. Tell them to get word to the troops. No one fires any arrows without an express order. Anyone who does will answer to Jathez' whip."

Rocca saluted, his gaze roaming down the short hill into the camp, looking for either one of the marshals.

Bree spotted Sandresin and nudged the big guard. "There, over by the king's pavilion."

Rocca nodded and made his way calmly down the hill.

Bree noticed how his steady demeanor calmed some of the more agitated soldiers among the newer recruits. Officers were forming their people into squads and she was pleased at the level of discipline most of her units displayed.

Leopold motioned for Bree and Eavan to join him as he made his way back to Taklishim's tent. He nodded to a sub-commander, who brought fist to chest as they passed, and spoke quietly to his cousin. "If nothing else, this will serve as an excellent training exercise. The sub-commanders, and the officers who answer to them, will be able to see where the weaknesses lie and fine tune their troops."

Bree noticed Liris and her squad of six positioned at a discreet distance at various locations around Taklishim's tent. Fully armed, they faced outward to guard against anyone fool enough to use the distraction to attempt to harm the Shaman or his warrior. Tisneé also stood guard outside the Shaman's tent, his knife sheathed at his waist and a battle-axe held loosely by his side.

The king noted them as well and sent an approving glance at Bree before nodding to Tisneé who stepped aside but didn't relax his vigilance.

When Bree and Leopold entered, Taklishim was sitting with Ebi's head in his lap, stroking between her ears. He looked up when they entered and waited for them to come sit on the log next to the fire.

Bree knew Leopold was in a hurry, but she also knew some Shona customs from listening to Becca speak of her experiences among the tribes. She took his elbow and motioned toward the log nearest the shaman.

He understood and once they were settled, Taklishim very calmly addressed the king. "Acoma tells me Nashotah and a few warriors are riding this way."

The king sighed. "And Acoma is?" He looked to Bree for clarification.

"His Spirit Guide."

"The same Acoma the bards sing about?"

Bree raised her eyebrows and slowly nodded.

Leopold looked at Taklishim with a feeling of wonder accompanied by a little bit of fear as well. If Spirit Guides really did exist, and he still harbored his doubts, then this man's Guide was a legend among his own kind. He couldn't believe he was actually asking the next question, but he took a deep breath and asked anyway. "Did Acoma say what they wanted?"

The old man shifted into a more comfortable position. "Denabi sent for Nashotah to help the White Wolf heal the Badger. Her wounds are—" He looked up into Bree's eyes. "Serious."

Sighing again, Leopold said to Bree. "And Denabi is the Black Panther the bards also sing about?" Bree nodded again, and he asked. "And she is the Spirit Guide for what venerable Shaman?"

Bree bit back a smile, anticipating her cousin's reaction. "My daughter, Kaiti."

Leopold's mouth dropped open.

Bree leaned over and whispered. "Close your mouth, Sire."

That jolted him out of his shock. He stood and walked to the opening of the tent. Before leaving, he turned to the Shaman. "Can I trust Acoma to know whether Bree and I can ride out to meet them without being filled full of arrows?"

Kalian, Nashotah's Black Leopard Guide, appeared next to Bree.

For some reason, Bree's ability to see and hear other Guides was expanding, but she was still surprised to see a Black Leopard, who wasn't Denabi, standing next to her and even more surprised when the Leopard addressed her. *I am Kalian. Nashotah sends her greetings and asks permission to enter your camp. She is waiting in the glade where the spring leaves the mountain.*

Bree remained silent, forgetting for a moment that the king couldn't hear the Leopard.

Taklishim relayed the message instead. "Kalian, Nashotah's Guide, says Nashotah sends her greetings, and asks permission to enter your camp. She is waiting in the glade where the spring leaves the mountain."

Bree looked from the Panther to her king, who was doing remarkably well considering the circumstances.

He simply shook his head and motioned to the tent opening with a wave of his hand. "Let's go then." When the two of them stepped outside, six horses awaited them, saddled and ready to ride.

Jathez sat atop a large, dappled mare, wisps of her storm-gray mane rippling in the slight, dawn breeze.

Darius held the reins of the king's stallion, Ruthless, whose muscular shoulders and flanks danced under a dark, well-worn saddle. The blanket beneath the saddle was trimmed with a maroon and metallic-gray crossover pattern that contrasted handsomely with the horse's sleek, obsidian coat.

Kaiti held Rebel, whose slightly confused pedigree was quite apparent in the presence of the other two noble beasts.

Eavan sat atop a bay gelding holding the king's standard—a flowing pennant, intricately embroidered with a powerful Mountain Goat standing with his front hooves elevated on a boulder.

Once the king and Bree mounted, two of Leopold's bodyguards mounted as well.

As they rode away, Bree glanced up to see Liris following her with her gaze. When she'd caught Bree's attention, the Estian raised her eyebrows and swiveled her head to the right, then back to Bree, sending a silent message before turning and facing away from the tent, once again keeping an eye out for trouble from the camp.

Not certain she understood Liris' intent, Bree studied the soldiers off to the right. One man, standing at attention in a nearby squad, stared at Tisneé with undisguised hatred in his eyes. He focused on Bree as she rode past, his lip curling in disgust.

Her eyes tracked to the man standing next to him. Yellow stringy hair fell to his shoulders. His chest-length beard held uneaten pieces of food and his filthy tunic showed a month's worth of grease and grime. His bloodshot eyes followed her as she rode by until he, too, shifted his attention to the young warrior standing ready to defend his chief— alone if necessary.

Other soldiers in the unit glared at the warrior; some young, some old, most unkempt and dirty. One woman, an archer, had her gaze riveted on the Shona tent. Her muscular hands hung at her side, clenching and unclenching as if preparing to fight an imaginary foe.

A prickle of unease ran down Bree's spine. She didn't recognize any of the soldiers and took note of the officer in charge, intending to tell Jathez to keep that squad out of her command. The officer wore his thick gray hair pulled into a knot at the nape of his neck. He was clean shaven, with a scar running from the side of his nose, across his cheek and back toward his ear. But most telling were the yellow stripes around his upper sleeve. Yellow was Guildenhall's colors, and, until recently, Jeffries had been the Earl of Guildenhall. Was the facial scar possibly a wound taken while fighting the Shona during King Pries' reign?

The officer noticed her studying his unit insignia. He flexed the muscles in his jaw before deliberately turning his back to her.

She looked to her left and saw that the king had his attention focused in the other direction. "Leo."

He turned, his eyebrows pulled low over his eyes, surprised that she'd use the familiar in this type of setting.

Bree pulled her horse to a stop.

In order to hear what she had to say, he had to stop as well. He side passed his horse close to hers, leaned over and said quietly, "What is it?"

Bree looked back at Liris who stood watching her again.

Liris nodded imperceptibly, once again raising her eyebrows. She slowly pulled her bow off her shoulder, slid an arrow from its quiver and held it down low by her leg.

Instinctively, Bree agreed with Liris' assessment. She turned back to the king. "Leave Jathez here, Sire. Something bad is going to happen if you don't."

"What? Bree what are you talking about."

Bree answered quietly. "Leave Jathez and send for Sandresin to bring a squad of soldiers he trusts to guard Taklishim."

Not sure what had Bree worried, Leopold stared into her eyes trying to understand her meaning. He trusted her uncanny intuition, which, at times, had saved him from not only the gleeful fury of his father's wrath but also from an ignominious death on the field of battle. Her instinct had also saved him from many intricately plotted deceptions when the two of them were young and learning how to survive the deadly games practiced by the nobility in his father's court.

He tapped his horse's flank with his spur and rode up to where Jathez patiently waited. "I need you to stay here. Taklishim is *your* direct responsibility. Nothing untoward happens to him while I'm away."

Jathez looked at Bree, his fingers absently stroking the leather reins he held loosely in his right hand. When his gaze returned to the king, the steely glint of determination that characterized his service to the crown could be seen behind his dark, deep-set eyes. "My life for his life, Sire. I swear it."

"I'll send Sandresin to stand with you, and we'll sort everything out when I return. If I return with the Shona," He took a minute to scrutinize the many ranks of soldiers, most of whom had their eyes riveted on their king. Tane's blood. They were *his* soldiers, and he trusted them, but Bree had rarely steered him wrong. "If I return with the Shona, watch for trouble."

Once he'd given his orders to Jathez, the king swiveled in his saddle and searched for his son. He found him standing next to the tent with Tisneé and Kaiti. He rode back to Kalsik, who stood off to the side, alert to any possible danger to his charge. "If there's a problem, take Darius and the girl into the forest until I return. When you see me, if my reins are in my left hand, return to the camp, if in my right, stay where you are. If there's trouble, ride for Cafria."

Kalsik nodded and looked to Nordin, who'd moved his hand to the hilt of his sword. "As you wish, Sire."

The king and Darius stared at each other for a long moment. Darius brought his hand up to rest on the hilt of his short sword, standing tall and straight as he waited for his father to leave. Feeling an unexpected burst of pride, Leopold gave him an approving nod before riding back to where Bree waited on Rebel. "Let's go find Sandresin. The last I saw him, he was over by the council tent."

He squeezed his legs and his horse started forward, weaving its way through the crowded encampment. White clouds drifted skyward as the breath from ten formations of thirty-five soldiers each met the cold, autumn air.

Marshal Sandresin was just coming out of the council tent when they approached. He quickly brought his fist to his chest.

The king didn't waste any time with the formalities. "Take two squads of your most trusted soldiers. Form up in front of the newly pitched healer's tent where Taklishim and his warrior are staying."

"Sire." Sandresin saluted again, and immediately left to hand pick twenty men and women from within the ranks of the soldiers standing in formation.

Leopold wasted no more time on Bree's suggestion. He'd done what she'd asked, and now he was anxious to meet with the Shona. Their arrival was an unexpected bonus as far as he was concerned. Taklishim was their undisputed leader, but the old man was living on Aevala's grace, and who knew how long that would last. If he could establish a rapport with one of their other chiefs, maybe he could continue to repair some of the damage his father had wrought during his genocidal reign.

As they rode out of camp and started into the foothills, he absently watched a vulture soaring gracefully above the hill they were climbing, its movements almost lazy as it caught the wind and rode the currents higher and higher until it was nothing more than a tiny pinprick against the rust-colored clouds flowing out from either side of the rising sun. They crested the rise and saw tiny sparkles of light shining off the ribbon of water that wound its way through the valley below.

Leopold glanced back the way they'd come, scrutinizing the placement of the peaks and valleys formed by the hundreds of tents flowing across the golden grassland. Multi-colored banners belonging to various nobles flew throughout the encampment, with his colors flying highest of all.

He remembered his father pointing to a similar encampment, from a hill not much different than this, extolling his twelve-year-old son with the hierarchical relevance of banner and tent placement. He'd spoken about why a king needed to keep the royal heel firmly rooted on the necks of the Anacafrian aristocracy, and of the importance of beheading those who dared disobey his wishes in order to ensure the obedience of the rest.

To Leopold's surprise, as he studied the layout of the camp, a horseman cleared the perimeter and spurred his mount into a full gallop, racing through the tall meadow grasses on his way up the hill to their location. When the horse drew near, he recognized it as the healer's roan, and he was soon able to make out the features and riding style of his cousin's friend.

He'd seen quite a bit of the young woman recently, first while she'd tended to Bree at Orinshire, and now, as she was quite often present during his meetings with Taklishim. He vaguely recalled her as a student at the Collegium. She'd been assigned as an apprentice healer in the Huntington's Cavalry during the war. Now, as he watched her skillfully riding up the hill toward them, he remembered her dark orange healer's tunic in the midst of several of the bloodier battles, controlling her horse with nothing more than a slight movement of her legs as she wove in and out of individual skirmishes, shield in one hand and medical supplies in the other.

Holding up his hand, he halted the group and waited for her to join them.

She slowed and trotted the last few yards to his position, coming to a full stop and saluting before turning and nodding to Bree.

Leopold stroked Ruthless' neck, wondering what explanation she'd have for chasing after them when he hadn't specifically asked for her attendance at this meeting.

"Your Majesty, Lord Commander Jathez sent me as a translator. He sends his apologies for not thinking of the need before you left."

Realizing he should have thought of that as well, Leopold acknowledged her words with a slight nod, then reined his horse around and started down the other side of the hill. He'd had so little time lately to get away from the politics and intrigue of court and he reveled in the rhythm of his horse's gait as it picked its way through clusters of rocks dotting the boulder strewn hillside.

Ruthless avoided the sharp edges with an agility bred into his bloodline by generations of men and women whose only purpose in life was to provide their royal masters with horses of superior stamina, speed, and strength. But Ruthless eclipsed even the best of those bred within the royal herds. Every so often a handful of truly great animals emerged, the likes of which only came along once or twice in several decades of breeding. These horses had an uncanny, almost supernatural intelligence rivaling that of the Spirit Guides spoken of in the Shona legends.

Ruthless was one of three born within Leopold's lifetime. A second had carried his father into the last battle of the Estian wars and had died protecting the king's lifeless body while he lay sprawled in the midst of a field that ran thick with rivers of blood. The third was being raised alongside his son and would one day carry Darius into battle in front of an army of his own.

The king's musings continued as they made their way down the hill, which eventually leveled out onto an open field, the far border of which ended on the banks of a slow-moving stream. When they reached the water, he turned east and followed the contours as it wound around the edge of the valley, eventually leading them into the sun-dappled interior of the Forest of Aeval.

Leopold had been hunting among these trees since he was a lad carrying extra arrows for Sir Banyon, who'd loved the hunt more than political intrigue, and who'd lavished the young prince with the same amount of love and affection he'd bestowed upon his own many sons and daughters. Leopold owed his sanity to Congreve Banyon. He hoped that he'd gained at least a small portion of the old man's wisdom and character to counterbalance the unbelievable arrogance and ruth-lessness he'd witnessed during his father's reign.

His thoughts turned to the canopies of the ancient trees as they blotted out the sun and darkened the little-known path they were following. Thick vines hung draped over branches, forming a twisted maze where he could just make out the shapes of various animals and birds nesting within their coils. A lemur stared out at him from beneath her camouflaged hiding place, and he had to stop himself from acknowledging her greeting when it appeared that she'd winked at him and smiled.

Making time to bring Darius into these forests suddenly flew to the top of his list of priorities. There were ideas and lessons to be learned that could only be taught here, where the abundance of wildlife and lack of civilization were more than simply stories told to his son as he tucked him in at night.

This was where Darius would learn to watch and listen; to really listen to a speaker rather than to simply trust the words spilling carelessly, or treacherously, from a courtier's mouth. Nature, rather than discourse, was the greatest teacher for a young boy, and he'd been sorely remiss in that aspect of Darius' education.

Ruthless sidestepped suddenly, and the king instinctively reached for his sword when he saw Bree jump, looking both alarmed and then irritated by degrees with one emotion following quickly on the heels of the other.

When Garan had come bounding over a fallen log, Bree's heart added an extra beat and she angrily glared down at the White Wolf, who patently ignored the warning. *They're in the clearing just ahead. Bodaway and half his warriors escorted Nashotah. Bodaway is in one of his moods. You might want to warn the king.*

He fell into step with Becca's roan, easily keeping pace with him. *Oh, and Nashotah says you've been away too long, and she misses your...how did she put it...*

Becca spoke quietly. "Never mind what she said. That's personal."

Garan shot her a wolfish grin before loping on ahead.

Becca relayed what he'd said. "Sire, Garan says they're just up ahead. Nashotah's there, along with Chief Bodaway and about seventy warriors." A shiver of anticipation ran through her at the thought of seeing Nashotah again. Her thoughts turned to her lover's warm body lying next to hers, and she wondered how late the king would keep them after dinner.

Bree turned in her saddle, a look of consternation on her face. "Well?"

When Becca refocused her attention and saw that the king had also turned her way, she knew she'd missed something important.

Leopold pulled his horse to a stop, stiffly staring at the trees while he waited for her to bring her roan abreast of Ruthless.

"I'm sorry, Sire. Did you ask me something?"

The piercing glare Leopold turned on her made her want to duck down in the saddle and ride back to the encampment with her tail between her legs. She lowered her eyes, knowing she should have been concentrating on the task at hand.

Leopold curled his fingers tightly around his reins, then loosened them before addressing her between clenched teeth, "There is a time for mistakes, Healer, and this is not it. Now, if you're through wool gathering, I asked you to tell me about Chief Bodaway. What should I know before I ride into the glade?"

While she thought about the upcoming meeting, Becca drummed her fingers on her thigh, a habit she'd had since early childhood. "Bodaway is a very proud, somewhat impulsive leader. He's quick to anger, but he's also willing to listen to counsel. He, Nashotah and Dahana, another chief among the Shona, all grew up together, and any perceived disrespect toward her, no matter how slight, will lead to a confrontation."

"Why is he here with so many warriors? From what I could see from the lookout at the sentry's position, there were nearly one hundred accompanying him."

"I'm not exactly sure, Sire, but I can make a guess. You have almost one thousand soldiers traveling with you. Granted, they're split into three legions and two of them are traveling separately from you, but I'm sure he's been hearing reports of the troop movements the entire time you've been on the move."

"So, he wants me to know he has quite a few warriors as well."

Becca let her reins drop and bit her lower lip while she thought. "I think so. There's a definite protocol I would suggest you follow when the two of you meet." She wasn't sure if she should be advising the king on protocol, so she sat and waited for his response.

Leopold studied her a minute before nodding. "Go on."

She cleared her throat and continued. "You should ride boldly into the middle of the glade and remain on your horse until someone comes to hold your bridle. When that happens, I'd recommend you jump down from the saddle instead of using your stirrups."

"Jump?"

"Yes. Once you're on the ground, keep your hand away from the hilt of your sword. I've noticed you tend to rest your off hand on it when you're standing or riding, and that's considered a challenge to the Shona."

Leopold took his hand from where it rested on his sword and settled it on his thigh instead.

"If Bodaway begins to walk toward you, which he should since you came to him, stride boldly up to him, put your right hand on his shoulder, and say 'Peace, Bodaway.' He has a rudimentary knowledge of the Anacafrian language. Whatever tension there is should ease after that, and we'll be invited to eat with them. From there, you take your cues as you would in any diplomatic situation."

The horses shifted with pent up energy while the king thought over Becca's instructions. He quieted Ruthless with a hand before voicing his main concern. "I don't think it would be wise to invite him and his warriors into our camp. How do I handle that without giving insult?"

"Bodaway's no fool, Sire. There was a reason he stopped so far from our encampment. I'm sure he knows that only Nashotah will return with us, and once that happens, he and his warriors will probably return to his camp."

She turned to the two guards. "You two will flank the king as he rides forward but stay mounted when he dismounts. When the king and Bodaway turn to go to where they've set up their temporary camp, wait for Lord Commander Makena and I to ride to your position."

Taking a minute to adjust his tunic, Leopold straightened in his saddle and the party began moving toward the glade. As they emerged from the tree line, they saw approximately seventy-five warriors mounted and waiting in a semicircle, with Bodaway and Nashotah sitting astride their horses in the center. Leopold rode forward, and Becca quietly spoke to Bree. "We wait here until the greetings are done."

The two guards rode past and took their places behind and to either side of Ruthless.

Eavan started forward, but Becca stopped her. "No, wait. Just stay here with the duchess and me." They watched as the king rode up to the semicircle and stopped. Ruthless, probably sensing the tension in the air, pawed at the ground impatiently, dancing in place to relieve some of his pent-up energy. His arched neck and flowing mane were an impressive sight, and Becca was proud of the way her king sat him so confidently.

Her breath caught when she looked past him and saw Nashotah sitting astride her bay mare, her beautiful half smile and laughing eyes greeting her across the field of waving grass. Becca returned her smile, then wrenched her eyes away to watch what was happening with the king. He'd been absolutely right when he'd said this wasn't the time for mistakes and she needed all her attention focused on the drama unfolding before her.

She noted Bodaway's barely perceptible nod, which was a sign for one of his warriors, Nugén by the looks of him, to dismount and approach the king. Nugén was a good man with excellent instincts and she was sure Nashotah had had a hand in his selection for this part of the greeting. He strode forward, took hold of Ruthless' bridle and respectfully waited for the king to make the next move.

Leopold waited a few heartbeats, then practically vaulted out of his saddle, landing squarely on his feet as though he never dismounted any other way. She heard Bree chuckle softly and stifled a grin of her own. The king nodded slightly to Nugén, who dipped his chin in response.

Bodaway handed his reins to Nashotah and dismounted. As he walked forward, the casual set of his shoulders belied the importance of this aspect of the meeting. In the Shona culture, if the king waited for Bodaway to come all the way to him, that was a clear sign of his disdain, and a challenge for the chief to either fight for his honor or acknowledge Leopold's sovereignty over him and his warriors.

When the chief had taken four or five steps, Leopold strode forward relaxed and unconcerned—the way a king would greet a fellow monarch—and placed his right hand on Bodaway's shoulder, just as he'd been instructed.

Bodaway returned the gesture, looking into the king's eyes for any sign of duplicity. When he lowered his arm and gestured with a sweeping motion indicating that Leopold should join him, there was a palpable wave of relief that washed over everyone in the glade.

The warriors turned their horses as one and faded into the forest where Becca knew they'd have a temporary camp set up. Judging by the sweet aroma wafting through the glade, Bodaway had brought along several women to prepare a venison and vegetable stew often served during ceremonial occasions.

She, Bree and Eavan rode forward to where the guards waited.

Bree turned to her, unsure of her next move, and Becca tried to put her at ease. "They have a meal prepared for us back among the trees. We're now honored guests. The king will sit on Bodaway's right, and you should sit on his left."

She turned to the two guards who were looking decidedly nervous at the absence of their king. "The two of you need to sit and eat with the warriors. King Leopold's life is now their responsibility, and they'll protect him from an enemy attack even before they protect Bodaway."

She gently kicked her roan forward, but before she'd gone five paces, Eavan trotted her horse up next to hers. "Should I stand behind the king like I do at the castle? Do I serve him his meal or sit with the guards or should I do something else?"

The barely noticeable quaver in her voice alerted Becca to just how nervous the young woman really was. She felt bad for not remembering the squire would feel completely out of her element here. "You're doing fine, Eavan. When we dismount, carry the standard with you into the camp. You'll see a spear stuck blade first into the ground. It'll have three feathers tied at the top. You need to stride over to the spear and if the dirt is soft enough, plant the standard next to the spear. Make it look easy, as though whatever you do is what happens every time. If you can't push it in deep enough so that it stands on its own, don't wrestle with it, trying to shove it in. If that's the case, I'm afraid you're going to have to stand there and hold it until we leave."

Eavan nodded as she listened intently to her instructions.

Becca could see that the squire understood the importance of the spear and the standard and would stand holding the staff all night if necessary, to uphold the king's honor. The healer also knew that having a definite roll to play had eased Eavan's fears somewhat, and she watched as the girl relaxed into her saddle as they rode forward.

When they reached the edge of the forest, the only person waiting for them was Nashotah. She'd dismounted and was standing next to her horse, her ebony hair rippling softly in the breeze.

Becca had helped her to learn Anacafrian, and when Bree

approached and swung down from the saddle, Nashotah smiled and respectfully lowered her eyes for a fraction of a second, as an equal would greet someone of their own rank. "It is a pleasure to have you as our guest again, Duchess. You have been away from our fires for too long." She paused, then lightly placed her fingers on Bree's forearm. "I haven't spoken to you since Timur joined the goddess on his walk. My heart grieved with yours."

The muscles in Bree's jaw flexed, but she answered as anyone trained in diplomacy from their time in the cradle, would. "Thank you. Becca brought me your condolences, and the herbs you sent helped more than you could possibly know."

In reality, Bree had thrown the packet of soothing florets back into Becca's face, choosing instead to wallow in her grief rather than take any comfort from Nashotah's kindness.

Bree knew that the two healers were anxious to greet each other properly, so once everyone had dismounted, she motioned for the two guards to join her and for Eavan to bring the standard and follow her into the woods. "If you'll excuse us, the king will be expecting me."

When they were gone, Nashotah met Becca's gaze, asking in a soft whisper, "Has it only been fifteen moons that you've been away from our bed?" She lovingly stroked Becca's soft cheek before running her thumb gently across parted lips. Moving close enough to feel Becca's heartbeat on her breast, Nashotah closed her eyes and breathed in the familiar scent of the Rowanleaf needles her lover used to soften the ground beneath her furs.

Becca's hands moved slowly up and down Nashotah's body, caressing her doeskin tunic and sending shivers of pleasure up her spine.

Their cheeks touched, and Nashotah reveled in the velvety smoothness she found there. Placing her hands on each side of her lover's face, she put her lips next to Becca's ear and whispered. "Tonight, my love. Tonight, I'll show you all that you've missed."

Becca's hunger grew as Nashotah's tongue slipped gently around and inside her ear, circling the place Nashotah knew was guaranteed to inflame and arouse.

Becca whispered, "I wish tonight was now, and I could lay you down on my furs and do delicious things with your body." She slid her hand between their bodies and gently caressed Nashotah's breast, delighting in the response she always found there. Sighing, she remembered her duties and reluctantly lowered her hand. "As much as I wish I could have you right now on this carpet of grass," She retrieved the reins she'd let fall to the ground. "We need to join the others."

Nashotah gave an answering sigh and gathered her reins as well. "I begged Bodaway not to come. You know how I hate posturing and politics, but he insisted it wouldn't be right for me to simply walk into King Leopold's camp without an escort." She chuckled. "Gitli wanted to be the one to take the king's reins, but I said I'd ride to Leopold's camp alone in the middle of the night if Bodaway agreed to that."

"Gitli? That man's heart is as black as the Teivaiedin. In fact, I'm sure the only reason he wasn't at the Battle of the Seven Realms with a black guide on his shoulder was because Muda had already knocked him senseless."

Before the battle, Dahana's son, Muda, had defended Nashotah's honor when Gitli and Tsoe had insulted her. Nashotah had been teaching him the art of spear fighting and after three years of her tutelage his prowess wielding the spear was second only to her own.

"I didn't even want him to allow Gitli to come, but he's one of the elders and had the right to join us. If he'd have taken the reins of your king, who knows what might have happened. Speaking of which," She turned and led Becca into the woods. "I think we should be at the dinner to make sure he behaves."

CHAPTER 7

W hen the two of them walked into the clearing, everyone had already taken their places around the fire. Becca was surprised at how elaborate the camp was given the short amount of time they'd had to prepare. There was something familiar about the setting, and she suddenly realized they'd come to the headwaters of one of the tributaries that fed into Príusin's River. If she'd been paying more attention while they were riding, she would have recognized this as a meeting place used by various Shona tribes whenever two or more factions needed a safe location to meet.

The trees here had been thinned to the point where a completely circular, manmade meadow sat tucked away in the middle of the forest. Becca realized the king must have known exactly where he was going since there were only two perfectly concealed entrances into or out of this clearing.

In the center of the open space, orange and yellow flames leapt skyward from a fire fueled by branches and tree trunks as thick around as the girth of a hibernating bear. A circle of logs surrounded the fire.

This was where Bodaway, Leopold, Bree and the elders ate; leaning against the logs and balancing their plates on their laps. They sat on animal skins laid out on the forest floor. Becca saw they'd brought the winter bear pelts that were usually kept stored away until they were needed for spiritual or ceremonial occasions.

Eavan had managed to firmly lodge the king's standard in the ground next to Bodaway's spear. Surprisingly, the Shona had placed a second spear next to the first. Becca walked over to examine it. As she drew near, she could see the intricately carved illustration Jiven's aunt had designed six months before Nashotah and her twin brother, Adené, were born. Two figures circled head to toe, one much larger than the other, had been expertly carved around the shaft, then colorfully painted with bright red, yellow and green dyes by one of the artisans of the tribe.

Jiven, Nashotah's apprentice, had an aunt who had the legendary gift of foresight. She'd foreseen the birth of the twins, and had a vision, which foretold that the smaller, Nashotah, would lead the larger. Her vision had turned out to be absolutely true.

Nashotah stepped up next to Becca and ran her hand along the shaft of the spear, feeling along the grooves of the carving with her thumb. "Beautiful isn't it?" She sighed and dropped her arm to her side. "The spear isn't something I wanted. In fact, I'd hoped the day would never come when I'd be presented with it."

"I don't understand. Does it have a special meaning?"

Before Nashotah could reply, Eavan walked over, bowing her head in front of Nashotah and waiting as she'd been taught during the cultural sensitivity training Jathez mandated for all pages and squires.

Becca spoke quietly. "The banner's placed perfectly. How's everything going over there?" The three of them turned toward the fire where several women and younger warriors were busy serving the food.

"It's going fine. There's a young girl who seems to be translating pretty well. I think she's missing some of the nuances, though. Luckily, when she does, it's pretty obvious and no offense is taken. It would probably be a good idea if you were there for the finer points." The beseeching look Eavan turned on her let Becca know the squire was still worrying about the protocols of the meeting.

As they watched, Bree and the king burst into laughter, followed soon after by the translator, who covered her mouth and turned in a circle, giggling with embarrassment.

Becca moved her head forward as she tried to focus on the girl through the smoky haze curling through the air between them and the fire. "That looks like Seshawah." She grinned at Nashotah, who had an eye on Bodaway to see if he found whatever had happened as amusing as the king.

He turned a stern eye her way.

"It is. I wonder what the little imp did this time." Shaking her head, Nashotah chuckled when Bodaway raised his eyes skyward, his characteristic dimple showing on his cheek, which, when translated, meant that the tiniest grin was trying to force its way past his usually somber appearance.

Eavan nervously rubbed her knuckles. "How old is she?"

"Ten, with the heart and mind of a twenty-year-old." Nashotah smiled at the squire. "Becca and I have been teaching her and Tisneé to speak Anacafrian, but I didn't expect her to try translating so soon. She's Tisneé's little sister."

Becca reached out and stilled Eavan's hand, effectively keeping the young woman from rubbing her knuckles raw. "Eavan. Look at me." When she did, Becca continued, "There's a reason you're the king's squire. You're competent, bright, and excellent with your sword and shield. You've been with Leopold when emissaries from other kingdoms have come to visit. This is no different."

When Eavan glanced up at Nashotah, she blushed. "I haven't met many Shona before. I've only heard stories about how fierce they are. I guess...."

Suddenly Becca knew why Eavan was acting in a totally uncharacteristic manner. "Oh...I understand. You're afraid that if they take offense, they'll attack us. Am I right?"

The blush deepened and Nashotah, whose name meant, "loving protector," placed her hand on Eavan's cheek. When Eavan looked up into her eyes, Nashotah smiled. "Peace, Child. We aren't the barbarians your previous king tried to make us out to be. We are fierce in battle, just as your king and his knights are fierce when they fight an opponent."

She stepped closer, placed her hand on the squire's shoulder and slid her other hand down until she held Eavan's chin cupped in her hand. "But, if Bodaway were to take offense at something you or King Leopold say or do, he'd simply gather up his warriors and ride back to his camp. He'd remember the slight the next time your king approached him about something, but no more than that."

She let her arms drop to her sides. "It's all a dance, Child. You simply have to learn the steps." Taking the young woman by the shoulders, Nashotah turned her toward the second fire. "Now, go and eat with the other warriors. They're no different than the young men you're used to. In fact, I've noticed some appreciative glances coming your way."

Eavan faced the healer, straightening her shoulders. "Thank you. I can see I've been acting a fool." A slightly more cheerful glint shone in her eyes. "I'm afraid I never was very clever on the dance floor." She smiled, then walked back to where the warriors and the two guards were sitting.

Nashotah sighed. "We'd better get over there, as well."

Becca reached out and stopped her friend. "Wait, I still want to know what this spear means. What did you mean when you said you were hoping it would never come to you?"

"It means they've chosen me to take Kayah's place as a leader among the tribes."

"Among the tribes? Plural?" Becca's eyebrows shot up into her hairline. Kayah was Taklishim's wife; a healer and a respected leader in her own right. "You don't mean just in Bodaway's tribe, do you?" Becca looked back at the spears. "That's why your spear stands higher than his, and why yours has four feathers instead of three."

When Nashotah nodded, Becca showed her white teeth in a teasing grin. "Does this mean I'm the wife of a chief now instead of simply the wife of a healer?"

Shielding Becca's body from the others with her own, Nashotah ran her fingers lightly up and down her lover's arm. "It means you have to obey my every command tonight when we're finally alone." With that, Nashotah turned and made her way to the ring of logs encircling the campfire.

Becca took one last look at the spear and then followed.

As they neared the group, two husky warriors left their places at the second, smaller fire and stepped up to one of the logs.

Becca had known Nugén since he first danced the warrior's steps three years earlier on his fifteenth birthday. He and the other young man each took an end and before Becca knew it, they'd lifted the heavy timber and placed it at a one-hundred-and-twenty-degree angle to the one Bree, Bodaway and the king were leaning against. That way they could all be comfortable and still conveniently see each other during their conversations.

Nashotah bent to pick up one of the bearskins and repositioned it in front of their log. "Thank you, Nugén, St'ena."

Both men nodded and returned to their places with each one casting a surreptitious glance at Eavan.

Becca chuckled as she watched St'ena flex his muscles more than actually necessary as he held on to the log behind him and lowered himself to the ground.

Seshawah and Muda, Dahana's son, brought them plates piled high with a colorful, roasted medley of vegetables. Reds and browns dominated, with sweet yellow kernels sprinkled throughout. Nestled in their midst were thick, orange salmon steaks still sizzling from the open fire, covered with blackened herbs and spices.

Becca glanced over and spoke to Bodaway. "You must have brought Asher with you. I'm surprised Dahana was willing to give up her cooking for even a few days. You honor us, Bodaway." She spoke in Anacafrian for the king's sake, knowing Nashotah would translate for her.

Everyone looked to the cook fire where a middle-aged woman checked more pieces of salmon that she'd wrapped in wide leaves and placed among hot coals.

Taking Becca's lead, Leopold picked a flake of fish from his plate and ate it, closing his eyes and sighing as it practically melted in his mouth. "I don't think I've ever tasted such an incredible mixture of seasoning herbs before. The woman has a truly wonderful gift to be able to mix such taste sensations for both the fish and the vegetables. The healer is correct. We are well and truly honored with a meal such as this."

Laughter rang out from the group of warriors as Nugén and St'ena playfully wrestled each other in the grass. After a short time, St'ena pushed to his feet and motioned to one of Leopold's guards, asking him to join them.

Both guards waved away the request until Leopold called over to them. "Go on Rocca. You might learn some new moves. It never hurts to spar with an unfamiliar opponent now and then."

Rocca cast a glance over his shoulder at the king. After he saw that Leopold meant what he'd said, he set down his plate, unfastened his bandolier and handed it to the other guard. He unstrapped the belt that held his shortsword and handed that to him as well. When he pulled off his tunic, several of the females, and a few of the males, stared appreciatively at his dark, well-muscled chest and arms.

The two men began circling, first to the right, then to the left.

St'ena darted in and grabbed Rocca's legs, trying to unbalance him.

Rocca went down on one knee and grabbed St'ena's wrist, pulling his body around and rolling to try to pin the man.

St'ena's strength was in his quickness and before they hit the ground he'd spun out of Rocca's grasp.

Bodaway watched the two men intently. He admired Rocca's obvious strength, which rivaled his own. One day he'd like to match his fighting style against the big man to see who could best the other. But he also knew St'ena was as quick as a cobra, striking quickly and pulling back to safety. Bodaway had wrestled with him on many occasions, actually being bested once or twice in the process. He watched a while longer before turning to the king. "I would ask you something."

Becca slid closer to the two men and quietly translated.

Leopold shifted around so he and Bodaway were face-to-face. "Of course."

"You have our greatest chief with you in your camp. His wish was to take only Tisneé with him even though I counseled him against going alone. Now, you will have my healer as well. I refused to give my permission for her to come, but my Guide, Hecla, told me otherwise." He glared at Nashotah, obviously unhappy with the decision. "I am placing great trust in you, King Leopold. What assurances do you give me in return?"

Just as Becca finished the translation, a roar went up from the warriors watching the match. Rocca had succeeded in pinning St'ena and was now holding out his hand to help the young man up.

St'ena, for his part, was grinning from ear-to-ear as he took hold of the proffered hand and jumped to his feet. He pounded Rocca on the back, then led him back to his seat and handed him his tunic.

Rocca thanked him with a nod and began to dress, first donning the tunic, the shortsword, and finally his bandolier.

In the meantime, St'ena took Rocca's plate to Asher and asked the woman to refill it.

Asher piled the plate high with vegetables, pulled a salmon steak from the fire, unwrapped it and settled it on top. She retrieved another packet and unwrapped a honey-glazed sweet bread, which she personally walked over and presented to him.

Rocca, usually a taciturn man, gave her one of his infrequent smiles as he settled in with the new plate of food, carefully setting the pastry aside for later.

Bodaway turned back to the king, waiting for an answer.

Leopold stared off into the distance while he formulated his reply. "All three of them—I include your warrior as well—are under my protection. One of my two lord commanders and my best soldiers are personally guarding Taklishim and Tisneé while I'm away from the camp. That is how seriously I take the safety of your people. I, and my people, will protect them as if they were members of my own family. I can't give you a better guarantee than that."

Bodaway nodded solemnly as Becca translated, and when she was done, he finished what remained of the food on his plate. The scent of the herbs Asher had sprinkled into the cook fire lay heavily in the air. A slight breeze picked up a pile of scattered leaves, twirling them merrily around the camp while the warriors and the Anacafrians finished eating the remainder of the food.

The meeting had gone well, better than the king had expected, but he was still relieved when Bodaway motioned to some of his warriors to bring Ruthless and the other horses into the clearing. Once they'd mounted, Leopold decided to broach a touchy subject. "There have been some threats to my kingdom. Taklishim believes that one day your warriors and my soldiers will have to learn to fight side-by-side. I intend to begin making plans for that day. Our ways of fighting are different, and there is still a great deal of mistrust on both sides." He paused and then pointed at his cousin. "You know the Duchess Makena. If you would agree, I would have her meet with you, or with another of the Shona, on a regular basis to devise a plan to train our people to fight together as one. Would you allow that?"

When Becca finished translating, Bodaway stood silently a moment, mulling over the king's words. After a short time, he reached back and pulled his spear from the ground. He wasn't quick to answer. In fact, he never answered.

The king watched as the chief left to join his warriors who were busy piling dirt on the fires and packing up the cooking supplies.

Nashotah smoothed her horse's black mane, which flowed down onto a seal brown coat. "Bodaway isn't a man who acts quickly unless there is a crisis. The fact that he didn't tell you 'no' is your answer for now."

The king continued to stare after the chief. After a few heartbeats, he pulled his horse around and nodded once to the Shona healer. "Fair enough." He kicked Ruthless into a gallop, the horse's massive muscles churning through the waves of autumn grass with more speed and grace than any of the rest who attempted to keep up, save one.

Nashotah's mare matched Ruthless stride-for-stride and Becca, who'd been watching the pair from the back of her galloping roan, called over to Bree. "She's beautiful, isn't she?"

Bree grinned at her lovestruck friend. "Who, the horse or the lady?"

In truth, both were beautiful to Becca. She heard Nashotah's laughter and watched as the two horses slowed to allow Eavan and the guards to catch up. Bree and Becca were bringing up the rear when Garan appeared and began loping beside them. *Trouble's brewing in the camp. I've been walking through the ranks listening to their talk. There's a small number of people who believe Taklishim and Tisneé should be hung instead of treated as honored guests.*

That was exactly what Liris had been alluding to by her cryptic messages, but it still bothered Bree that Garan had heard people actually threatening Taklishim. She called down to the big Wolf. "Jathez is there. I don't think there's any immediate danger."

Jathez has relaxed his vigilance since nothing has happened. He's sent half his people to the cook tents. Garan suddenly tripped as he looked back over his shoulder.

Bree "heard" a yelp in her mind as he tumbled head first onto his chest and then rolled and came up with a mouthful of grass. They'd pulled up short after his tumble and he glared at them balefully after spitting out a mouthful of greenery. *If you say anything...*

Becca raised her eyebrows, smothering her laughter in her hand.

Bree simply chuckled and rolled her eyes. "So, you're the noble Spirit Guide, huh? Very impressive."

Garan glared at Bree before holding up a paw toward Becca. *I'm wounded.*

"Where?" Becca dropped her reins and was just about to jump down to check him when he replied.

She has wounded me to the core.

Bree snorted while Garan wiped dirt off his ear with his front paw. He finished getting the dust out of his coat by shaking his entire body, beginning with the tail and ending at his ears. *Oh, I almost forgot the most important part. When Kaiti was walking through the camp, she saw a black guide on one of the bearded men. By the time she reached Taklishim to tell him, she was no longer able to find the man or his Teivaiedin.*

That was enough to get Bree's attention. "Let's go." She kicked Rebel into a gallop and she and Becca easily caught up with the others who'd slowed to a steady trot.

Nashotah and the king were discussing the events of the day and the others had fallen back to give them some privacy.

Bree and Becca rode up and matched the pace of their horses with Ruthless and Nashotah's horse, Esul. "Sire, Garan says trouble's brewing back at the camp."

"And Garan is...the healer's Spirit Guide?"

"Yes. He says he overheard several soldiers saying they thought the Shona should hang. He also says Jathez has sent half his contingent to the cook tents to get their midday meal."

"He overheard—" The king looked directly into Bree's eyes. "So, these Spirit Guides spy on my people, then report back to their...what are they called?" He turned to Becca for clarification.

"Apprentices."

"And then they report back to their apprentices. Why does that make me extremely uneasy?"

Bree pursed her lips. "In truth, it makes me uneasy as well, but that's something we can discuss some other time. The point is, we need to get back to camp as quickly as possible."

It had taken them about two candlemarks to reach the rendezvous and Leopold nudged his horse into a steady, ground eating cantor. This was a gate Rebel could maintain for several candlemarks, and he easily stayed by Ruthless' side while the king continued to ask questions. "Is there any way we can get a message to Jathez?"

Nashotah, who rode on the king's left, grew animated as she answered. "That's exactly why Taklishim hopes to help you. If you and Jathez were open to your Guides, communication would be so much easier. Then Garan wouldn't have to act as a messenger boy between you and Jathez."

Messenger boy? I am hardly a messenger boy! Garan had been loping beside Becca, but he moved up to run next to Nashotah. *I do both you and Denabi the favor of taking my own time to come and—*

"Peace, Garan. I meant no disrespect. I'm trying to put things into terms King Leopold will understand."

Well that I can understand. These last few generations of apprentices haven't really been overly bright.

The sparkle in Nashotah's eyes as she glanced back at Becca was almost as comical as listening to Garan's complaints. Once again, Becca found herself hiding a smile as she turned her face away from the White Wolf. She'd been busy trying to figure out a way they could get a message back to the camp. They could tell Kaiti, but Becca knew it was highly unlikely Jathez would listen to her.

If they told Tisneé, he might have his Guide, Azeel, report back to Bodaway, who would come stampeding into camp to "rescue" Taklishim. "I suppose Garan could take a message to Taklishim, who could relay it to Jathez, but honestly, I don't think Jathez would take him seriously. If you don't believe in Spirit Guides, and he doesn't, then there's no reason to believe Taklishim has a message directly from King Leopold."

No one spoke as they entered the forest and became somewhat separated. They each took their own paths through the dusky interior, where the sunlight shining down through the thick, intertwined branches gave the fallen leaves a shadowy, dappled appearance.

Becca watched as Esul effortlessly flew over a downed log. She pointed her roan in the same direction, but apparently, he thought the log a little too high for his taste. He balked, and she went flying forward onto his neck. She held on for all she was worth and cussed a blue streak that would have made even the most hardened soldier proud.

Nashotah laughed as she heard Becca's angry curses. She pulled Esul to a walk and brought her back to the log. The horse and rider stared over the trunk at their friends who by now had repositioned themselves for a second try.

The healer moved Esul to the side while Becca and the roan gallantly rode forward in their second attempt at jumping the downed tree. Nashotah smiled at the looks of determination both horse and rider wore as the roan lifted his front feet off the ground and sprang forward on bunched hindquarters to soar, almost effortlessly, over the tree.

They galloped determinedly after the king and Nashotah joined them, whooping a Shona battle cry at her friend's success. She called across to her lover as they raced through the trees. "I'd say I'd give you a Shona battle horse so you didn't have to ride the roan, but he has such a huge heart I don't know how you could do without him. His embarrassed expression after he balked was priceless."

The group exited the forest and rode across the meadow and into the foothills and were soon wending their way up the boulder-strewn hillside. A sentry's whistle announced the return of the king.

Leopold slowed to a fast walk as they rode past and the man pounded his chest in salute.

Becca recognized him as a veteran of the Estian Wars, a tree-line reconnaissance man with eyes as sharp as an eagle. Unbeknownst to him, his Spirit Guide, the Stepit Eagle, Torsal, often assisted in his spying duties. Becca caught his eye, and he gave a quick nod and an even quicker wink in return.

As Bree rode by, he saluted her as he'd saluted the king, and she nodded absently in his direction.

A horn sounded in the distance, somewhere in the vicinity of the camp, and the sentry swung around in surprise. "Summat's wrong a'ta camp, Highness."

The king turned Ruthless in a circle. "I heard it, Arnis. Keep a sharp eye."

Ruthless leapt forward as the king released his steadying hold on the reins and once again, he and Nashotah led the headlong dash; this time with a sense of urgency rather than play.

Becca urged her roan to his fastest speed, leaning forward in her saddle and holding the reins loosely on either side of his neck.

Bree pulled in front of her as Rebel kicked into a mad dash, sensing his rider's need to arrive in camp close on the heels of her royal cousin.

The two guards also passed to either side of Becca, more desperate than Bree to keep up with Ruthless in order to protect the king.

Eavan, carrying the standard, brought up the rear, grumbling that the standard bearer and guards should have horses that could outpace the king's, so he didn't go tearing into battle without his banner or his protection.

As they drew near, the clash of swords could be heard along with angry shouts of men and women running toward the disturbance.

Nashotah and Leopold galloped into camp before the others. They found Jathez and a handful of his soldiers defending Taklishim's tent against a cadre of some thirty attackers.

Without a moment's hesitation, the king and Nashotah thundered into the fray. Ruthless and Esul moved into battle mode, teeth and hooves ready to protect their riders from whatever enemies approached.

Leopold fought from the saddle, blocking a sword to the left while Ruthless swung around to put his hind hoof through a second man's throat on the right.

Becca and the two guards reached the camp a few moments later. They knew their priority and all three raced to protect the king.

A wiry, unkempt soldier managed to evade Ruthless' hooves while a second attacker fought Leopold from the front. The man's thin appearance belied a sinewy strength and agility which he expertly used to his advantage. He twirled into Ruthless' flank, leaped up and wrapped both arms around the king's shoulders, pulling him backwards and down toward the ground.

Knowing the king was much safer when mounted, Becca kicked her roan forward until he rammed sideways into Ruthless, trapping Leopold's leg between the two horses. She dropped her sword and wildly grabbed for the king's tunic, somehow managing to wrap all ten fingers in the heavy, quilted material. When she felt she had a solid enough grip, she immediately pulled backwards with all the panic and fury she possessed.

Ruthless realized her intent and miraculously shifted his weight down and under the king.

Even as he was being jerked this way and that, Leopold expertly reversed his sword and thrust downward under his armpit driving his blade deep into the man's exposed throat.

Seeing the man attacking from the ground, Rocca leapt from his saddle and ran to Leopold's side. He literally tore the man loose from the king's blade, flinging him viciously to the ground before turning and blocking a killing blow from another man's battle axe.

Becca had jerked so violently on the king's tunic that when Rocca tore the man free, both she and Leopold overbalanced in the other direction.

The king sprawled across the roan's withers, but in an instant, he shoved himself upright, somehow maintaining control of his sword. He caught Becca's startled expression and gave her a fierce, triumphant grin before kicking Ruthless back into the fray.

Becca's sword lay in the dirt beneath her roan's hooves and she had no means to defend herself. An attacker noticed her lack of a weapon and closed on her from behind. Seeing the look in the man's crazed eyes, she kicked free of her stirrups, swiveled around and used the roan's hindquarters as a springboard. She threw herself at the man, wrapping her arms around his shoulders and ramming her head into the underside of his chin. The two of them sprawled backwards onto the ground, sliding on the blood-soaked earth before coming to rest against the outer edge of a small cook fire.

Becca looked around wildly for a weapon. Not finding any, she rolled onto her back and seized the man's sword arm with both hands to keep him from running her through.

The man shifted to the left, pinning her under him. He brought both knees onto her shoulders to hold her still and grabbed a knife from a sheath on his belt with his free hand.

Kicking her legs up, Becca wrapped her knees around his head and flipped him onto his back.

Obviously skilled in hand-to-hand combat, he used their momentum to continue the movement until he was once again above her. Just as he pulled his arm back for a killing thrust, a staff whipped across his forearm splintering the bone with a sickening crack. A second killing blow to the head stopped the man's pain-wracked scream before it fully formed.

Shocked at the sudden turn of events, Becca blinked up at Nashotah as her lover turned to engage a hulking woman wielding a halberd. Grabbing her attacker's discarded sword, Becca ran to join Jathez and his soldiers fighting to hold the perimeter against a fresh onslaught of traitors.

Nashotah finished off her opponent and then ran to augment Liris' people who were guarding both Kaiti and the entrance to Taklishim's tent. She assumed a back-to-back fighting stance with Tisneé, who wielded a long-handled hatchet with deadly precision. A yellow-haired man whose crazed expression showed pure hatred for the Shona healer immediately swung his large broadsword directly at her neck.

She ducked and used her staff to block and redirect the blow. Before the man could recover and swing again, his expression turned to shock and then to disbelief when Nashotah reversed her swing, slashing across his nose and breaking it before reversing her momentum once again. She rammed the end of the staff into his nose, driving the bones into his brain, killing him instantly.

Off to Nashotah's right, Bree had been forced to dismount and do battle from the ground. Rebel had no battle experience and was more than simply worthless in a fight, he was downright dangerous with all of his panicked flailing about. When she'd jumped from her saddle, skirmishers had immediately surrounded her, and she found herself fending off two battle-scarred women who were obviously used to fighting as a pair. She'd managed to parry a slicing jab to her midsection when she heard an unmistakable, high-pitched shouting above the normal din of battle.

She dodged a second strike by the woman on her left, slipped in under her exposed arm and drove one of her knives deep into the tall woman's chest. As the dead attacker slid to the ground, Bree pulled another knife from her bandolier and whirled to her right intending to finish off the second attack. Before she had the chance, one of Jathez' guards used his longsword to deliver a vicious blow to the side of the woman's neck, neatly severing her head from the rest of her body.

Dragging her gaze away from the fountain of blood spurting from the stump that used to house the woman's head, Bree frantically searched the vicinity of the tent where she'd heard the familiar voice yelling a series of commands. She saw Kaiti standing behind a human wall made up of Liris and her soldiers. They'd formed a semi-circle around the tent opening and were fighting a pitched battle against a handful of Guildenhall's infantry who'd gotten past Jathez' outer perimeter.

With her back to the guard who'd come to her aide, Bree took a moment to look at what held Kaiti's frantic attention. Garan and Denabi twirled in what appeared to be a battle with nothing but air. Claws unsheathed and teeth bared, they slashed and snarled at an invisible enemy.

Kaiti yelled another warning to her friends, "It's a bear, Garan! Denabi! It's a bear!"

Her shout brought Bree's attention back to the child just as Kaiti pushed between her protectors and attempted to run help her friends. She watched Liris make a wild grab, snatching the collar of Kaiti's tunic and throwing her backwards into the center of the semi-circle. Luckily, Liris recovered at the last second, dropping to one knee in time to parry a killing blow from her opponent. She blocked the downward stroke and managed to spin quickly on her heels, capturing her opponent's sword arm between her body and upper arm. She drove her sword upward, forcing the tip through the man's chin and watching as it exited the top of his skull.

Liris lost a few seconds fighting to pull her sword free, but by that time, Bree had run into the fray. She struck down a man who obviously intended to run Liris through with a rakeborn pike; one of the deadliest hand-to-hand fighting weapons in all the kingdoms.

Kaiti remained oblivious to everything around her except for Denabi and Garan, who'd adjusted their fighting tactics now that they knew their opponent was a bear. She watched the black beast pull back a huge paw, preparing to rake his claws across Denabi's exposed chest and neck. Kaiti screamed a terrified warning. "Denabi! Down!"

The Panther immediately dropped to her belly.

The razor-sharp claws missed taking her head off by mere inches. The Teivaiedin pulled his massive arm back to swing again, leaving his underarm completely exposed. Ready for his move this time, Kaiti screamed again. "Now, Denabi! Jump forward and bite hard!"

Denabi immediately pushed herself forward with her powerful hindquarters, massive incisors bared and ready to strike. When she felt her mouth connect with fur and flesh, she tore into the bear's underarm, ripping through his exposed artery.

The enraged bear roared just as Garan, taking his cue from Denabi, leapt up and clamped his jaws around the bear's jugular, ripping it in two.

The bear fell sideways, its blood gushing from the severed arteries. With the life force leaving its body, the black Teivaiedin faded until Kaiti could no longer make out the contours of its massive silhouette.

Garan and Denabi continued to whirl this way and that, ready for another attack.

Kaiti called out to them, "He's gone! You killed him."

While the Spirit Guides were battling their assailant, Liris was fighting a mountain of a man who'd succeeded in delivering a glancing blow to her left shoulder. Even though she managed to turn away most of the force of the strike, the power behind the attack forced her backwards. Her heel caught on a body lying at her feet and she fell backward, landing with a jarring crunch that took the breath from her lungs.

Anticipating a deadly follow-up blow from her opponent, she automatically brought her sword up to a defensive position and braced for the blow that never came. Instead of continuing the attack, the man dropped like a stone. She watched in confusion as his eyes glazed with the glassy stare of death before his body fully hit the ground.

Kaiti yelled across to her. "His bear's dead! He's dead!"

Liris had no idea what the child meant about a bear, but she could plainly see that the man was, indeed, dead—even though there were no lethal wounds on his body. By this time, enough of the soldiers loyal to the crown had flooded into the area and by shear, overwhelming numbers they'd brought the fighting to an end. Most of the attackers lay dead or wounded around Taklishim's tent.

After they'd caught their breath, Jathez and Bree began issuing commands, returning some semblance of order after the chaotic battle.

With blood dripping from the point of his sword, the king remained in his saddle, glaring down at the traitors while trying to fathom the reason for their insane behavior. Surely the fact that he'd banished their baron was no justification for treason.

Kaiti, who still stood behind Liris, saw a familiar, deadly motion out of the corner of her eye. She turned to see a woman behind a wagon aiming an arrow directly at King Leopold. Time slowed as she watched the woman's drawing fingers extend, releasing the projectile with deadly skill and precision. Without thought for her own safety, Kaiti sprinted forward and dove into its path. To her shock, as she flew through the air, a throwing knife came slicing past her ear, driving deep into the woman's right eye. The force of the blow jerked the bow skyward, sending the arrow harmlessly into the surrounding treetops.

Time moved back to normal for Kaiti as she plowed face first into the dirt, sliding forward and under the wagon, finally coming to rest with her body halfway beneath the undercarriage. She lay there a moment catching her breath.

Big hands grabbed her legs and pulled her backwards. Startled, she turned onto her back and saw Rocca standing over her, a fierce look of pride etched onto his features. He reached under her arms and picked her up, holding her dangling in front of him with her legs about two feet off the ground. She flinched as he roared at her, "Theur saved th' king!"

Turning her so she faced outward, he lifted her high and spoke loud enough for those around him to hear. "Th' bairn saved th' king. Me life fer 'er life!"

A cheer rose up as soldiers raised their fists and echoed the big guard's words. "My life for her life!"

While Rocca put a thoroughly confused Kaiti on his shoulder and paraded her through the camp, Liris stepped next to Bree who'd gone whiter than a snow goose's down. "I've never seen anyone throw a knife with that kind of accuracy before." She shook her head slowly. "Tane's blood, Duchess, you're good."

As Bree turned her way, Liris grabbed an arm to keep her from falling. "Whoa, you look like you're ready to faint. Come over here and sit down." She tried to lead Bree to a nearby log, but the duchess pulled her arm away and straightened.

"I'm fine. I was just afraid—" She stopped midsentence and watched as Rocca set Kaiti back on her feet. She could tell the little girl wanted to get away from all the cheering and was relieved when Becca walked over and put her arm around Kaiti's shoulders. "My fingers slipped a fraction of an inch, Liris. I...I almost put the knife through Kaiti's head...I almost—"

Liris put her hand on Bree's shoulder and stepped in front of her. "Here now, Duchess. You saved her life and the life of your king. Your daughter is fine, and she's a warrior you can be proud of. When Kalsik saw there was trouble, he grabbed Darius and Kaiti and headed for the forest. Kaiti fought and kicked until he had to let go. She ran into the tent and came out holding a knife, ready to protect the shaman." Liris turned and watched as Becca lead Kaiti back to Bree's tent. "I have a feeling that someday, I'll be following her into battle." She smiled at her commander. "And I'll be happy to do it."

Bree took in a long breath and let it out slowly. "I saw you and your people protecting her. Thank you."

Liris bowed playfully, the sun's rays dancing in her eyes. "Our pleasure, Your Grace." She turned on her heel and headed into the interior of the camp, greeting several soldiers along the way.

Bree smiled slightly as one of the men pounded Liris on the back, a huge grin lighting his face.

One-by-one, Liris' followers gathered and sheathed their weapons before following her back to their tents.

Leopold walked up and stood next to Bree. "Incredible throw, Cousin. I'm indebted to you, yet again."

A little color had returned to her face and Bree gave the king a half-smile. "We're getting too old for this, Leo. I am anyway. Are you sure Desdamea is headed this way? Because if she's not, I'm ready to go home."

Sighing, Leopold crossed his arms over his chest. "You know better than anyone, Bree, I'm a man of peace. But I have to protect my people. She's coming, and with a large enough force that if we're not careful, she might succeed in her scheme to rule both Organdy and Anacafria and use our kingdom as a jumping off point to attack Estia from two fronts. I..." He turned slightly toward her. "*We* can't let that happen."

He looked up to see Kalsik, Nordin and Darius come striding out of the forest. Darius walked with his head high and his shoulders back as though nothing untoward had happened. He came and stood beside his father, who rested a hand on the boy's shoulder while Kalsik stepped in front of the king and saluted.

"We took up guard in the forest as you ordered, Sire. I tried to bring the girl, but she fought and kicked until I lost my grip. I knew I had to protect the prince, so it was my decision to leave her behind." He bowed slightly to Bree. "My apologies Duchess, but my first responsibility is to Prince Darius."

Bree nodded. "I understand, Kalsik. My daughter can be bull-headed at times."

Leopold chuckled. "Just like her mother." His attention turned to Nashotah as she helped Tisneé limp into the healer's tent. "We'd better go see to our guests. Join me, Cousin?"

As Bree followed the king, they stepped around several bodies littering the area where the battle took place. She noticed that the officer who'd been in charge of the traitorous unit now had a bigger scar than the one running along his cheek. His entire head had been cleaved in two, most likely by the halberd that was the weapon of choice for the Chite.

"Leo." Bree spoke as they dodged two soldiers who'd come to help collect the bodies. "There's a big, red-headed Chite I've seen around camp."

"Aren't all Chites big and red-headed?"

She smiled. "They are, but I'd like to have this particular one in my troops. I'd like to assign him as a bodyguard for Kaiti."

"Are you talking about Nordin's tentmate, Ranr? I have no problem with that. I don't think they've ever been in separate divisions before, but they'll do what needs to be done."

Before they entered the tent, Leopold gestured to Kalsik. "Please make sure Darius gets something to eat before he returns to my tent. Also, find Commander Shirin and tell her I said to assign two people she trusts to guard the Shona, then tell her I want her to set up rotating shifts. We'll be leaving in the morning, but I want a guard on them at all times." When Kalsik saluted and turned away, the king stopped him with a hand on his arm. "Make sure it's understood, we're protecting them, they are not our prisoners."

When Kalsik nodded, the king and Bree ducked inside the tent where Tisneé was arguing with the healer about needing care. "I'm not hurt, Nashotah. Nothing you can help with anyway. I was caught on my thigh by the flat of a sword. My leg's cramping, that's all. I should be outside on watch, not in here with you."

Taklishim still sat near Ebi who was watching Bree through bleary eyes. The shaman spoke quietly to Tisneé, "Rest, my friend. I still walk in this realm thanks to you and the king's soldiers, even though I had to fight a delirious Badger to keep her from battle." He stroked Ebi's fur while she in turn clacked her teeth in anger.

My place is in battle when a battle is at hand, yet you keep me here like some invalid. If you were anyone else, I'd have bitten your hand off your arm and spit it out on my way out of the tent.

Leopold, who couldn't hear Ebi, knelt next to the shaman. "You have my apologies. The dead wear the colors of the marshal I sent away."

"There was no harm done. If any of your people need a healer, Nashotah will help. Now, if you don't mind, an old man needs his rest."

Tisneé moved too fast as he went to assist Taklishim, causing his leg to spasm painfully.

Bree grabbed him in time to keep him from falling into the fire pit.

He smiled sheepishly and then lowered himself onto his cot.

Nashotah helped Taklishim lie down on his sleeping furs.

Once Bree had settled Tisneé as well, she and Leopold left to help with the aftermath of the skirmish.

When they emerged into the sunlight, they saw Jathez striding through the camp, the lines on his angular face tightly drawn across sharp cheeks. His stride was long and sure as he stepped past soldiers who recognized his anger and quickly moved aside or stood and pulled on their forelocks, a less formal salute than a fist to the chest.

The scamp who worked for the cook hurried to bring a kettle full of water through the camp, dodging tent poles and guy wires while staring at the water, trying not to slosh any over the rim. Fortunately for him, Jathez saw him coming and quickly pulled back, glaring at the boy who had no idea he'd almost run into the Lord Commander of the Imperial Guard.

The cook knew it though and came storming away from her cook fire, planting herself firmly in the boy's path with her fists anchored solidly on her generously padded hips.

Everyone in the nearby vicinity could see what was about to happen, and they all stopped to watch.

Bree heard Leopold whisper under his breath. "Uh oh."

True to course, the boy plowed into the cook, spilling water down the front of her dirndl skirt and completely drenching his own sandy-brown tunic and trews. He bounced off her as though he'd rammed into the battlements of a fortified castle and landed smack on his backside.

There was a collective intake of breath as the cook slowly held the soaked skirt away from her legs. The woman, who'd been unaware she'd had an audience, glanced up to see a large group of onlookers watching and waiting for her reaction.

Scowling, she shooed away the onlookers with a quick wave of her arm. "Aw, aam nay gonnae eat th' loon fur breakfast ye gawkers. Gang back tae yer wark an' lae us tae oorselves. Th' Kin' an' th' two laird commanders excepted, ay coorse." She pulled the boy up by his collar. "Yoo're lucky it was me ye drooched an' nae th' laird commander, ye wee scamp. Noo, gang fill th' pot again, an' watch whaur yoo're walkin' oan th' way back."

The boy scrambled up, grabbed the kettle and turned to run back to the stream, once again almost crashing into Jathez on his mad dash out of the camp.

Jathez stepped back to avoid another collision, shaking his head as he continued on his way to the king with Cameron following close on his heels.

Leopold motioned for them to join him as he and Bree wended their way to the royal pavilion and stepped inside. Once they were all within the canvas walls, the king angrily turned toward his lord commander. "Report, Jathez. I want to know what happened and how you let things get so out of control while I was away."

Drawing himself up straight, Jathez pulled on the bottom of his tunic to straighten any stray wrinkles and looked his king squarely in the eye. "I take full responsibility, Sire. After you left, I put together a squadron of ten, and told the rest of the divisions to fall out. We, the seven new recruits, and Sandresin's people stood guard around the tent as you ordered."

There was an angry glint in his eyes as he recounted the incident. "Nothing happened for several candlemarks, and I believed whatever had worried you had passed. I allowed Sandresin, his soldiers and five of my people time for the cook tents and told Liris to take her people as well. She asked if that was an order, to which I replied it was not. She ordered her people back to their positions and refused to leave. Thank Aevala she did, because shortly after that, we were overrun by that filthy squadron from Guildenhall."

Looking down, he angrily swiped at blood spatters staining his leather armor. "Luckily, they weren't only filthy, they were poorly trained as well. My five remaining guards, plus Liris and her six, and that young Shona warrior, fought an extremely bloody battle. Luckily, all of the remaining defenders were veteran soldiers who knew the most efficient methods for killing large numbers of people." He shook his head angrily. "Those fools. We killed many of them ourselves, but when you and the others came to our aid it was a bloodbath."

The king listened intently, letting Jathez tell the story in its entirety without interruptions. When the lord commander finished, Leopold glanced at Cameron, then back at Jathez. "If not for Liris and the other six supposed *cowards* who walked into our camp, you would have been overrun and Taklishim dead. If that had happened, I would have been facing Desdamea *and* a full-scale Shona uprising with my Imperial Commander lying dead on a bloody battlefield—killed by men and women he was supposed to be commanding."

He ran his hand through this hair. "Tane's blood, Jathez. I don't need to reprimand you because I've known you long enough to know you'll be harder on yourself than I would ever dream of being." Leopold walked to a flagon of wine, poured three glasses and handed one to Jathez and the other to Bree. "How many casualties?"

Cameron straightened and gracefully pulled a notepad from a small belt satchel. He opened to the correct page and pointed to an entry with a long, almost feminine finger. He cleared his throat before reciting the numbers he'd gathered. "Twenty-two soldiers from Guildenhall, dead. Two more gravely wounded." He lowered the pad and looked over the pages at the king. "I spoke with the healers. They're not expected to live through the night." He returned to his numbers. "Three others are wounded but expected to survive, and there are another three with no wounds at all."

He grasped the top of the page between thumb and forefinger and fastidiously turned the page. "Nineteen were from Guildenhall, three from Merimeadow, in Danforth," He glanced up at Bree before continuing, "The remaining eight were from Marblefort Downs, which isn't surprising since they're so close to—"

Jathez interrupted him. "Leave the speculation, Cameron. Stick to the facts, please."

"Yes, of course, Sir. I'm...let's see..." Blushing, Cameron once more took refuge in his lists. "Four of the king's soldiers were killed and seven wounded. All seven are expected to make full recoveries." He carefully folded his sheets and dropped them back into the pouch.

"Bring me the names of all of our men who were killed and wounded. I need to know if any of our dead had family traveling with us."

Cameron nodded primly. "I'll have that for you before the candle reaches the next mark, Sire."

"Jathez, I know Entis was the sub-commander under Jeffries, and as such, it would normally fall to him to command the rest of their troops. Unfortunately, I never liked the man and don't trust him. I want the remainder of the Guildenhall contingent dispersed among the rest of the army, with the exception of the remaining six who attacked you tonight. Put them under guard. I'll hold a tribunal in the morning and pass judgment on them at that time."

"And Entis?" Jathez didn't trust the man either.

"He should have been keeping a closer watch on his people after I dismissed Jeffries, not to mention the disgraceful state his troops were in when they arrived. Strip him of rank and send him back to Duke Brycon with a thorough description of today's events and of the state of Guildenhall's troops. In fact, send one of your spies as well, preferably someone of noble birth, to find out what's going on in Deerford. Brycon is well over eighty. If his duchy has fallen into disrepair, I want to know about it. Guildenhall is one of the largest cities in Deerford. Find out why Brycon allowed Jeffries to let his troops fall so far below an acceptable military standard."

Not for the first time, Bree studied Leopold closely, listening to the sound of his rich baritone as he rattled off orders and made decisions without the slightest bit of hesitation, or more importantly, without any hint of condescension.

During their childhood, she'd often hidden behind thick damask curtains and listened to King Pries bark orders at servants and military commanders alike with a disdain he leveled on anyone who came within his sphere of influence, including his only son.

Shaking herself out of her reverie, Bree signaled to the king that she was going out to check on the aftermath of the uprising. At his slight nod, she pushed open the flap and stepped out into the cool night air.

CHAPTER 8

The soldier, a burly, grizzled man whose nose hooked down and to the side, bit down on the leather strap while Becca pulled the last stitch through the deep gash in the upper part of his arm. She'd been as gentle as one could be while pushing a needle into someone's flesh and pulling it through to the other side. "Didn't I hear Kalsik tell you during sparring practice to keep that left arm turned away from your opponent when countering a righthanded downward slice?"

The man pulled the strap from his mouth and used the bloody sleeve of his tunic to wipe away the sweat streaming down his forehead. "He tol' me a'right. Bloody fool I em not 't've learned t' lesson." He flexed his injured arm.

Judging by the painful grimace, Becca guessed he'd never forget to pull his left side back before beginning his counter swing again. Two other healers were tending a woman with a belly wound, but other than that, it looked as though everyone else had already been taken care of. "That should do you. Make sure to watch for infection over the next few days." She nodded to him and walked to the washstand where she rinsed blood from her arms and hands.

Satisfied that she was as clean as she could get, she slipped behind a hanging partition and pulled on the clean clothes Eavan had thoughtfully brought for her. Not too far away, she recognized the voice of an old friend pontificating on the treachery of the Guildenhall traitors. Curious now, Becca ducked around the blanket and took a moment to see if he'd been hurt during the attack.

When she'd first arrived to help with the casualties, Healer Astig had ordered her to care for a young man who'd somehow fallen and dislocated his shoulder on his way to help Jathez. At the time, she hadn't paid much attention to the other patients, but now she spotted her friend laid out on a cot at the other end of the tent. She stepped over to one of the healers to ask how he faired.

"Well, to hear him tell it, he stopped a clumsy downward stroke of a pike with his left forearm instead of with his sword or shield. Broke the forearm, but he'll heal just fine."

Becca walked over to her friend. Tiny, crisscrossed scars lined his face—badges of honor worn by veteran soldiers who'd seen more than their fair share of battles. His green eyes tracked her progress as she made her way to him.

"I see someone's set your arm, Hayden. Do you need something for the pain?"

"Naw, th' healer lass gave me some potion or t'other a while back. Should kick in soon." He grimaced as he flexed several fingers poking out from the end of his cloth bandage. "It all happened too fast. No time t' grab m'shield. More's the fool me. Dumb luck that bastard was sloppy with th' pike or m'fool head woulda been bashed in."

Becca grinned affectionately. "Again."

A crooked half-smile acknowledged the truth of her words. "Aye, again." He lifted his chin, scratching his day-old beard with his unin-jured hand. "Was that yer lady frien' came whooping in with a staff an' saved your own noggin then, Healer? I've heard 'bout the Shona an' their battle skills. All I can say is I'm glad she weren't the one trying t' brain me.

Becca felt blood rushing to her face. She hadn't realized her love affair with Nashotah had become general knowledge.

Hayden threw back his head and laughed, then cradled his injured arm when the movement jarred the broken bone. When the pain passed, his usual ready smile reappeared. "Ah, yer blushin' something fierce, Healer. You've been with her a coupl'a years now, right?" He waited for her reluctant nod. "Ya think sumpin' like that won't get back to yer friends? I say git goin' to see her an' make up fer lost time."

It wasn't as though she hadn't almost exclusively thought about Nashotah for the last several candlemarks. The healing she'd done had been automatic; suturing and binding were skills she could perform in her sleep.

Hayden noticed her woolgathering and grasped her arm, turning her toward the tent opening with a gentle shove. "G'wan. You're not needed here any longer. I know if m' wife Canta were here, you wouldn't catch me with m' britches still on."

Only those who'd known her for any amount of time could get away with teasing her like that. After she'd taken a few steps, she called back over her shoulder. "If Canta was here, your trews would be the least of your worries after going into a battle without your shield. She'd skin you alive and hang your hide from the pole in the middle of camp." As she walked out, several of the others took up the teasing and Hayden amiably traded barbs with each of them in turn.

Once outdoors, Becca headed for her tent, intending to drop off her healer's bag before going to find Nashotah. As she drew near, she caught the hint of a familiar, unmistakable, musky scent. Whenever they made love, Nashotah would burn a medley of herbs and spices, unintentionally, or perhaps intentionally, conditioning Becca's body to respond in predictable and very pleasurable ways. She took a moment to pull the scent down deep into her lungs, inhaling the subtle hints of prairie lupin, peritin foxtail, and that elusive, something, that made her smile at the pleasant memories it evoked.

When she slipped through the opening of her tent, her first view was of the contours of her lover's shapely back, lithe and lovely beneath a fawn-colored robe. Becca watched as Nashotah gracefully knelt to light a small brazier at the far side of the tent. Off to the left sat a second scuttle, already lit, with thin trickles of smoke rising from three hollow spires.

Nashotah spoke over her shoulder. "I hoped you wouldn't be tending your patients all night. That would have been such a waste of some very rare, very effective herbs." She stood and faced Becca with a playful, knowing look in her eyes.

There was very little Becca loved more than staring into Nashotah's dark, sensual eyes. A few steps brought her close enough to slide her hands to the small of the healer's back, pulling gently until their bodies touched, her lips brushing across Nashotah's cheek as she whispered softly in her ear, "Holding you is all I've thought about since I first saw you in the glade."

Nashotah pulled her into a loving embrace. "I've missed waking to your smiling face in the mornings." She ran her hands along Becca's back and neck, then gently pulled away. "You've always carried your stress across your shoulders. Has it been such a difficult time with Taklishim?"

She lightly grasped Becca's arms and turned her. When she began kneading her shoulders, Becca tried to turn back, but her lover held firm. "Your shoulders feel like a taut rope, my love. Here, come sit on the furs." Becca knew she'd get nowhere until Nashotah had taken the time to relax her muscles and calm her spirit. Sighing, she obediently eased herself down and sat cross-legged while Nashotah massaged away the aches and pains of the last few days.

The healer eased Becca's tunic from her shoulders, then slowly unwound her chest bindings. After a moment, heated oil ran down Becca's back and breasts. As gentle hands began massaging the oils into overwrought muscles, the stress of the last few days slowly melted away. The tension in her muscles eased under Nashotah's loving ministrations.

Strong fingers slipped through the oils, squeezing and rolling, and every so often brushing over nipples and breasts, sending tiny sparks of pleasure radiating from her stomach to her inner thighs.

With silky hands, Nashotah guided Becca forward until she lay face down on a fur-covered blanket. As she settled quietly onto her stomach, Nashotah reached around and untied the bindings that held her trews. She moved down and removed Becca's knee-high boots and then slowly eased her leggings over her hips, pulling them down and off her outstretched legs.

Becca whispered, "How do you both relax and excite me with nothing but your touch?"

Once again, the oil ran; down her spine, between her legs and onto her calves and feet. Nashotah caressed her toes, tenderly working out the aches before moving up to her arches, her strong thumbs sliding deep into the soles of her feet, squeezing places that that sent spasms of desire racing through Becca's body. Hands slipped over calves and rode up the full length of Becca's thighs.

When Nashotah's thumb brushed over her skin with the gentleness of a feather's touch, Becca caught her breath, moaning softly as the feather continued its caress. She listened to the soft rustle of her lover sliding her robe down over her shoulders, and felt it pool on the ground next to where she lay.

Becca's breathing grew harsh as Nashotah ran her nipples through the oil on her back, first sliding up and around, then back down the full length of her body. Nashotah's soft breath called to her each time her lips brushed past her ear. Rising gently, she slid her thighs on either side of Becca's hips, rubbing herself in the oil until Becca wanted to cry out with the longing coursing through her body.

Finally, her lover lay on her and whispered, "Now, my love. Up."

When Becca rose to her elbows, Nashotah slipped under her, lying on her back beneath Becca's body. The passionate hunger in Nashotah's eyes mesmerized her.

Each rise and fall of Nashotah's breasts matched the desire building between Becca's thighs. Becca slid one of her lover's nipples between her legs and began rocking on a breast slick with hot oils that smelled of arousal and lust. When Nashotah put her hands on the small of Becca's back and pulled her forward, Becca covered her lover's smiling lips with her body, her passion exploding as those lips took her and caressed in time to the pulse of her beating heart.

CHAPTER 9

In the morning, Becca awoke to the banging of tent poles as the army went about the routine of breaking camp in preparation for the final leg of their journey. Three-quarters of them would split off toward various locations along the Cascadian Sea, while the king took the rest directly into King City.

It was a comfort to feel the heat of Nashotah's breasts as they pressed against her back. Becca caressed the hairs on the healer's arm draped possessively across Becca's side and breasts. "How long will you be staying?"

Nashotah kissed the back of Becca's neck. "I wondered how long you'd be able to sleep surrounded by such clumsy packing. If a Shona warrior made that much noise when breaking camp, he'd be run out of the tribe."

She rolled onto her back and sighed. "In answer to your question, I'll be able to stay only as long as it takes Ebi to heal. A few days at the most. Bodaway said he would send Nugén and St'ena back for me at the next new moon."

Rolling onto her back, and then onto her side, Becca turned and faced her friend, resting her temple on her raised fist. "I don't know if I can return with you. Apparently, the king has made Bree one of his lord commanders while he prepares for the possibility of an invasion from Organdy, and she may ask me to—"

"Invasion?" Nashotah sat up. "Is that why he's been gathering his soldiers?" The muscles in her jaw rippled. "That's what your king meant when he said there have been threats to his kingdom." She pushed to her feet and began gathering up the furs, angrily rolling them into a neat bundle. "No one bothers to let the Shona know what's going on. One of the reasons Bodaway came with me was to see if he could find out the king's intentions."

That made more sense than Becca cared to admit. It hadn't occurred to her that the Shona might be concerned about the legions of men and women traipsing across the countryside in answer to the king's call. She stood as well, picked up a length of rope and began to wind it around Nashotah's bundle. "I'm sorry, Shota. I should have sent word once Taklishim and I caught up with the army and discovered what was happening. Since the army had nothing to do with the Shona, it never occurred to me that the hotheads might twist it to their advantage. Are they calling for war?"

"They are. Bodaway and Dahana have had their hand's full countering the rumors that Leopold's gone back to his father's ways. That's why we had to have a meeting at the gathering place, and it's why that idiot Gitli had to come along." Nashotah turned and practically threw the furs into the corner.

Taking Nashotah's hands in her own, Becca made her lover look her in the eyes. "I really am sorry. There was so much happening here, I didn't think about what might be happening among the tribes."

Nashotah's piercing gaze softened. She took a deep breath and let it out with a sigh. "It's good to be sharing our furs again. I always watch for your return, and little Seshawah gives me a daily report from the scouts about whether they've seen you approaching." She smiled. "I think she misses the lessons in sword fighting you've been giving her."

Kaiti's voice carried into the tent. "Becca? Can I come in?"

Becca quickly grabbed her clothing and began pulling on her trews. The women of the tribe were perfectly comfortable being naked in front of the female children, but she hadn't quite adapted to that particular tradition.

"Wait for me to put some clothes on, Kaiti. I'll be right out." She heard an answering giggle and knew Kaiti had never understood why she and Bree never let her see them without their clothes.

Nashotah chuckled as well before handing Becca her tunic. She stepped closer and laced the cords that held up her trews. "I helped you out of these, it's only fair I help you back into them." When she'd finished, she pulled on her own robe and reached back to open the door flap.

When Kaiti saw the headwoman, the color drained from her face. She quickly ducked her head and stepped back.

Nashotah's eyes narrowed as she studied the girl. The child had been mistreated among Dahana's people, and numerous times either she or Adené had needed to treat her wounds or see to her physical needs. But now, circumstances had changed, and the child needed to change as well. "Are you Denabi's apprentice?"

Her tone was sharp and Kaiti flinched at the words.

The child didn't answer, and Nashotah took a half step forward. "I asked you a question."

When Kaiti's head moved in an almost imperceptible nod, Nashotah reached out and grasped the girl's chin, forcing it off her chest and up high enough so that Nashotah could look into her eyes. "The apprentice to one of the most respected Spirit Guides in the Seven Realms neither cowers nor hides her head in shame. Stand tall and proud when you meet me or one of the chiefs, show respect, but show us that you are to be respected as well. You are no longer their trash and you are no longer the Anacafrian's Dado. You are Denabi's apprentice and you must demand respect for her, even if you can't bring yourself to demand it for yourself."

When Nashotah glanced outside over the child's head, she saw the duchess standing a short distance away watching them. The woman's eyes held the dangerous set of a Badger's rigid glare just before it attacks a menacing foe.

Nashotah looked back at the girl who hadn't moved. She growled low in her throat, knowing she needed to force the point home to the child. "Stand tall, Kaiti Makena." She released her hold on her chin and glared down at her.

Slowly, hesitantly, Kaiti straightened her shoulders and looked Nashotah fully in the face before turning and addressing Becca. "Shimaa says you need to join her in the king's tent."

Becca, who'd been nervously watching Bree, nodded. "Tell her I'm on my way." The only reason her friend hadn't stormed over to tear Nashotah's head off was because of the healer's standing among the tribes and because of her relationship to Becca.

Kaiti glanced up at Nashotah again, dipping her chin slightly out of respect before turning to rejoin her mother.

Becca turned to her friend. "What was that all about?"

"The child's first response is to cower when she sees one of the Shona. You know the derision she faces among the tribes when she returns. And she will return. She must if we're to defeat the Teivaiedin, and she must return with her head held high or it will be a disaster for my people."

"She's been through a lot."

"Aevala knows that if a sapling withstands the harsh winds that seek to destroy it, when fully grown, that tempered wildwood will tower over lesser trees that grew in safety behind the protection of a sheltering rock. It will withstand even the most violent tempest because of the strength it gained while still that small, wind-battered tree."

Becca stiffened at Nashotah's words. "You're not suggesting that the horrors she lived through while she was Dahana's *property* were a necessary evil, are you? That she was somehow destined to be beaten and starved and humiliated?"

Nashotah's stiff resolve withered somewhat. Her shoulders sagged as she answered Becca's question. "No, absolutely not. My heart broke each time I went to Dahana's camp and saw her. You know I tried to bring her into my tent as my own, but you also know she was a gift to Dahana from Loneh. Gitli and Taima wanted her dead and Taklishim convinced me that the only reason she was allowed to remain alive was the fact that she was Dahana's property. If I had taken her in, it would have meant a death sentence for her."

Nashotah crossed her arms as if to brace herself from the truth.

"No child should have to go through what she did, but the fact remains, she not only survived the abuse and neglect, she was tempered by it."

Denabi's form began to coalesce beside the two women. Her muzzle came to the midpoint of Becca's chest, and she tilted her head slightly to address the healer. *There's one point you must understand, Healer. Not ever, not once, in all the time I've been her Guide and Guardian, has she ever felt sorry for herself. That is not part of her belief system, and it should not be part of yours. She is strong and must call upon that strength years ahead of when others usually mature. Both Nashotah and the duchess understand this, and, in order to help the Spirit Child, you must understand as well.*

Becca watched as Bree ducked into the king's pavilion.

Kaiti lingered a moment to pat the head of one of the camp's wild dogs.

"But why her? Why this bright, brave, loving little girl? Why not Dahana, or Bodaway, or even Nashotah? Grown warriors who've been proven in battle?"

The big Panther lowered her hindquarters to the ground and watched Kaiti as well. Her ears flicked once as she thought out her response. *There is a certain...I guess you might call it...magic, in the Aevalian Gifts. You have no way of knowing that through the generations, the number of people with the stronger Gifts increases or dwindles depending upon need. I don't mean the number of people who can see and hear their own personal Guides. I mean people who can see and hear all Guides. Those Aevalian Gifts, as the Shona call them, are controlled by magic, and not by Aevala herself. She created them, but only fate and circumstance control them.*

The three of them watched as Kaiti disappeared through the tent opening. *When Taklishim came into this Realm and Acoma became his Guide, we accepted him as this generation's bearer of the Aevalian Gifts. Normally, only one shaman per generation is so blessed. When Nashotah was similarly blessed, we believed she would one day take Taklishim's place. It wasn't until you, also, began to see and hear all of us, and the duchess began to see Garan before she even acknowledged Ebi's existence, that we began to wonder. Even more astounding, I was called to mentor a youngling in this First Realm; something that hadn't happened to me in ten generations. It was then that the gods began to take notice.*

Becca heard panting behind her and turned to see Garan lying in front of her tent with one paw casually crossed over the other. The side of his mouth quirked up in his approximation of a grin. *You do know that only the best and the brightest become Guides for those with the Aevalian Gifts.*

A sound that sounded surprisingly like a snort came from deep within Denabi's chest. *Yes, and we know that mistakes are occasionally made.*

Ha! Garan gave a wolfish laugh as he rose and came to sit next to Denabi. *Seriously though, Sheyah, Denabi's right. The child has a fierce sense of pride and loyalty, and she has a destiny. Your pity is misplaced—and dangerous.*

"I don't pity her, I—" Becca tilted her head to one side as she thought about her feelings for Kaiti. She felt protective of all children she came into contact with, more so if they were being abused. But did she pity them?

The White Wolf's striking blue eyes studied her. *Nashotah is strengthening the child by forcing her to acknowledge who she is and who she needs to become. You, on the other hand, want to shelter and protect her. You can't move the sheltering boulder to protect the sapling. You can support the little tree against the terrifying winds of Tane'iel, but you must let the trunk bend in order for it to be strengthened.*

Just then, Becca saw Kaiti run out of the king's tent.

The girl slid to a stop when she saw Becca looking her way. She frantically waved at her, while at the same time pointing to the tent opening. "Tane's blood, I forgot I was supposed to go with Bree to see King Leopold." She took off running, dodging soldiers along the way and sidestepping Kaiti who had a particularly worried expression on her face. "Thanks, Kitten."

When she ducked inside, the king, Jathez and Bree were standing next to a table on which the cook had laid out a somewhat smaller version of the hearty breakfast usually enjoyed by the king and his officers.

Jathez set his plate on the table and growled his greeting. "Are you in the habit of ignoring a royal summons, Healer?" The hard voice of command brought her to attention. Healers weren't soldiers, but they knew and followed the precepts of military discipline.

"No sir, my—" She judiciously stopped short of saying that her Spirit Guide had been explaining a point to her.

Bree watched as Garan strolled in and sat next to Becca. He blinked at the duchess. *Is there a problem?*

Bree pursed her lips and glared at him while Becca tried to ignore his presence.

Jathez scowled at her. "Your...what?"

Nashotah followed Garan in and calmly strode to a fruit platter laden with a variety of colorful, mouthwatering selections. She picked up a small berry and rolled it between long, elegant fingers. "Her Spirit Guide and I were discussing the fate of your kingdom and of my people. I apologize if our discussion delayed her."

Jathez leveled his steely gaze on Nashotah who returned the look in kind. When he opened his mouth to speak, Leopold silenced him with a hand on his shoulder. "These are stressful times, Jathez, and we all need to learn to adapt." His eyes flashed a dangerous warning when he turned his full attention on Becca. "However, we've spoken before of your priorities, Healer. Nothing," He turned his piercing gaze to Nashotah, "and no one takes precedence over me. Is that clear?"

There was nothing Becca could do other than nod. "Yes, Sire."

Some hair had fallen down over the king's forehead and he brushed it back into place with an irritated swipe. "For reasons totally beyond my understanding, Commander Makena will be staying here while I move on to King's City. She's told me she's staying until that..." He waved his hand in dismissal. "Badger recovers. Apparently, it's necessary that you remain as well."

Becca acknowledged his words with a nod but said nothing.

"But that's neither here nor there. I've called you in to discuss the medical repercussions that might occur from the facial branding of the seven new recruits since I intend to accomplish that this morning before I ride out. I'll be leaving them here with you while they recover from the burns."

It had been difficult enough for Nashotah to remain silent while her partner was being chastised, but when the word "branding" left the kings lips she almost choked on the berry she'd just eaten. "Branding? You intend to take a hot iron rod to some of your soldiers in order to mark them as you would mark a horse or valuable dog?"

Very little the king could have said would have shocked her more.

She pushed past Jathez and confronted Leopold with an outraged expression. Nashotah continued speaking, or rather, attempted to speak, but was having a difficult time actually formulating her words. "You...you...I can't believe..." She drew herself up to her full height, which didn't begin to match Leopold's rather tall six foot three. She nevertheless looked quite imposing. "And you call my people barbarians!"

In Anacafria, no one berated the king, ever. Becca knew that Nashotah had only known a limited number of Anacafrians during her lifetime and had learned about their culture from them. At Nashotah's request, Becca had tried to teach her about political hierarchy and the absolute power of kings, but her friend's limited grasp of the concept was reflected in Bree's startled expression and Jathez' indignant intake of breath.

Leopold's jaw clenched as he glared back at the Shona healer, but his innate sense of diplomacy and good breeding kept his answer mostly cordial. "Not that I have a need to explain myself to you, Healer, but in this particular case, I will. I have no other choice but to alter their marks. They were wrongfully branded as cowards in another country, and I have pardoned them. If I leave the "C" burned into their cheeks without altering the letter to something less damning, they'll be beaten and stoned in any city they come to."

Blinking, Nashotah realized how incredibly different their two cultures actually were. She glanced at Jathez, whose apoplectic expression told her just how very far she'd overstepped her diplomatic bounds.

Taking a deep breath, she laid a conciliatory hand on the lord commander's shoulder. "Peace, Commander Jathez. Some of your culture's practices are so foreign to the Shona way of thinking that I forgot myself for a moment." She smiled, "Now, please breathe before you damage yourself."

Leopold chuckled and patted Jathez on the back. "Easy my friend. I appreciate your anger on my behalf, but it is completely unnecessary. I assure you my honor is fully intact."

Becca watched Jathez make a conscious effort to regain his composure. There was nothing subtle about the way he bought himself time by jerking his tunic straight and twisting his head from side to side trying to loosen the whipcord tight muscles in his neck. "Yes, Your Majesty. We...I need to remember that Nashotah and Taklishim are bound by different rules of propriety and decorum, and as such, a perceived lack of respect is only a perception and not necessarily a reality."

When Becca's eyebrows shot up in surprise at Jathez' unexpected eloquence, his eyes softened somewhat and an amused expression—albeit one that would still terrify the most junior of his officers—came over his face. "Yes, healer, I have slightly more education than that of a common soldier."

For the first time since Becca had come into the tent, Bree entered into the conversation. "Jathez is a first-tier scholar in the King's Collegium and teaches Philosophical Abandonment when his military duties allow."

Becca hoped her astonishment didn't show. She carefully schooled her features to a more neutral expression. She'd known Jathez was of noble birth. That was a given since he was one of the king's imperial commanders. However, most nobles received a rudimentary education at best, choosing instead to learn the machinations of court politics while others, like Jathez, studied military tactics rather than pursuing more advanced studies at the King's Collegium. But a first-tier scholar as well? Very few full professors attained that level of learning, and she'd had no idea that the irascible, hard-bitten Marshal Jathez was that far advanced in his studies.

With a pensive expression that Becca knew only too well, Nashotah turned and retrieved another piece of fruit from the bowl. "Could I possibly suggest an alternative to your dilemma?"

Leopold walked over and took a sprig of red berries for himself before shaking his head sadly. "I've wracked my brain trying to find a way to protect these people. They're honorable, brave soldiers who didn't deserve to be disgraced in the first place and who don't deserve to be branded now. There is no other option, Healer, although I thank you for offering to help."

Nashotah took Becca's forearm in her hand. She turned it face up to reveal the identifying symbol every Anacafrian baby had tattooed on the inner side of their right wrist. She let Becca's hand drop, then in succession did the same to Bree and Jathez, and finally to the king. All of them had very detailed drawings on their arms showing exactly which alliance and which duchy they'd been born into. "Use these skills to alter their scars."

The solution was so obvious and had been overlooked simply because the tattoos had only ever been applied to newborn babes, never to an adult. Unless of course that person lived in or was personally acquainted with the fringes of society. No well-born Anacafrian would ever think of getting the base, lowborn markings worn by the common bumpkin or dockhand.

An almost palpable relief washed over the king when he realized he wouldn't have to brand Liris and her people after all. "Brilliant." He turned directly to Jathez. "Do we have any midwife artisans accompanying us?"

"No, we had no need since none of the soldiers or camp followers were with child."

"We'll have to send one back from King City then. I don't want them entering the city without their new markings. I want you to tell the soldiers accompanying us to the castle garrison to spread the word that those seven have been pardoned and are under my protection. Have them regale their friends in the taverns about how honorable and brave their new companions have shown themselves to be. Tavern talk gets the word out better than any royal decree."

Turning his head away from the king, Jathez bellowed, "Cameron!"

The young man put his curly head through the tent opening. "Your Grace?"

"Tell all of the heralds to meet with me before we leave."

"Yes, Your Grace." He ducked back out of the tent.

"Oh, and Cameron."

This time the squire stepped completely inside. "Sir?"

"I need the list with the names of the six remaining traitors."

A large leather satchel hung down near Cameron's thigh, cleverly attached by a strap worn diagonally across his chest. A second strap threaded through loops that ran the circumference of the top of the bag. This circled his waist and reattached to the satchel, thus rendering the entire contraption not only inviolate but immobile as well. The flap was tastefully, and Becca noticed, expensively, decorated with multicolored, filigree embroidery. She recognized the work as that of the Thadon Artisans who made their homes in that duchy's Gilded Forest.

When he opened the flap, Becca could see that the interior had been carefully designed with the life of a traveling scribe in mind. Intricately organized pockets of every conceivable size and need lined all four sides of the interior. No expense had been spared in its design, and not for the first time Becca eyed the squire with an intense curiosity about his lineage.

Cameron produced a carefully folded piece of parchment and handed it to Jathez.

"I made you a copy with the names of everyone involved in the insurrection, Your Grace." He began to take the parchment back, presumably with the intention of unfolding and translating its contents. "You'll notice—"

Jathez snatched the parchment away and made shooing motions with it. "Go, Boy. Do as you've been told. I think I can figure out who is who on the list."

Blushing, Cameron bowed to Leopold and nodded to Bree and Jathez on his way out.

Bree, who was well acquainted with the rigors of life as a squire, waited until he was out of earshot. "You shouldn't be so hard on the boy. He's doing his best."

Jathez grimaced. "I know. He's my brother's wife's nephew. The boy has wanted to be a knight ever since he was old enough to talk, but you've seen him. Some people are born soldiers, others are born scribes or archivists. Give him a sword and he does more harm to himself than to his opponent."

Nashotah had trained many young warriors in her time. Many of them had been ill suited to conventional weapons, but once she'd matched the weapon to the warrior, all of them had excelled. "Have you tried him on any other types of weapons?"

"I don't have time. I put him with weapons masters who throw their hands in the air after only a few lessons. I use him as my scribe, but…" He trailed off, believing the futility of the task was obvious to everyone present.

"If you would allow it, I'd like to work with the boy. I can see he has the heart but perhaps not the build for conventional weaponry."

Looking first to the king, and then to Bree, Jathez finally shrugged his approval. "If you can turn him into a warrior, I'd be eternally grateful. And if you can take some of the popinjay out of him, even better."

Nashotah looked to Becca for translation. "Popinjay?"

The only way Becca knew to translate this particular word was to give an example. "Do you remember Kolnath, in Chethan's tribe?"

"Ah." Nashotah's face lit with amused understanding. "A man with the body of a flamingo, and the heart of a warrior." Her eyes took on a far-off look, which Becca knew meant she was already planning Cameron's future. "I'll only be here until Ebi heals. Can the boy remain behind while you ride on with the army?"

For just a split second, Becca thought she saw relief wash over Jathez, but he quickly schooled his features into his usual, taciturn scowl. "Of course. I have an older page who can take up Cameron's responsibilities. He can return with the duchess after she's taken care of…whatever it is she's dealing with."

He'd never actually seen Ebi, and no one had offered to explain what was happening in Taklishim's tent. The particulars really didn't matter to him as long as they didn't affect the orderly running of his Imperial Guards.

"Now," Leopold steered the meeting back to order. "About the matter of the six traitors. They took up arms against my army, which means they took up arms against me."

His voice took on a harsh tone. "They're to be hanged before we leave camp. See to it."

He spread his hands as he addressed Nashotah. "Hanging may seem barbaric to you, but we've discovered leniency for certain crimes only breeds contempt."

"If you knew how Bodaway punishes those who plot against him, you'd have your proof that we are indeed a savage and brutal people."

Leopold stared into Nashotah's eyes long enough to see the truth to her words. "I suppose we're all barbarians in our own way. So, I know you came to help with the Badger, and I assume you're staying here while Taklishim accompanies me to King City." He began listing people on the fingers of his right hand. "Bree, you'll have the healer and Kaiti and Nashotah with you."

"Becca."

"What?"

"The healer's name is Becca." Bree smiled at the look Leopold turned on her. "And I'd also like the Chite to stay with us."

The king made a dismissive gesture with his hand. "Yes, fine, he's yours."

Jathez, who'd been reading the list Cameron had given him, looked up. "I've assigned Arnis and two of his sentries to remain behind, as well as Lorek and his squad.

When Bree opened her mouth to protest, Leopold held up his hand. "I know you can take care of yourself, Cousin, but with reports of assassins in the land, you'll need to humor me. You'll also have Liris and her people here, at least until the midwife can alter their scars."

Bree knew there was no sense in arguing with the king once he'd made up his mind. There was only one more problem she'd been trying to see her way around. "I was hoping to get back to my steading to make sure everything is all right there. I left in a rush quite a while ago, and while I know Becca arranged for a family to take care of things, I'm still somewhat worried about my animals."

The king rubbed his chin while considering Bree's request. "I need you with the army, Bree. I'll be in King's City half a fortnight, no longer, and then we're moving on to the coast. There's no telling when Desdamea will make her move, and I can't afford to have half my army without their lord commander."

Bree tried to focus on the sounds of the soldiers as they dismantled the camp instead of on her frustration. She heard the king muttering to himself and turned her attention back onto him.

He shook his head as he spoke. "I can't believe I'm saying this," He turned a quelling look on Jathez. "And if you let even a hint of this get out to the troops…"

Jathez' thick eyebrows rose up into his hairline, but he said nothing.

The king ran his hand through his hair before looking directly at Bree. "Can you ask the healer's Guide, Garan, or whatever his name is, to check on your steading and report back to you?"

Ha! An amused bark sounded in the corner, but Bree refused to turn and look.

Jathez shot an incredulous glance at the king, whose cheeks had turned a slight shade of pink.

Leopold waved his hands in front of him. "Never mind, forget I said anything. Perhaps we could send a messenger to go take a look."

All the women in the tent hid their amusement while Jathez once more schooled his features into neutrality.

Bree decided to come to the aid of her king. "One of the soldiers in Lorek's squad is the youngest son of a man who owns a good-sized farm near Ashton Fork. I'm sure he'd be more than happy to make a quick visit to his family, and he's more than qualified to check on my steading for me. If that meets with your approval, I'll send him later today."

"Of course, that's fine." Leopold's voice was a bit deeper, more masculine than usual. He turned to Jathez. "Pass the word that we'll be leaving within the hour. As we discussed earlier, I want you to accompany the troops who are heading straight to Port Suliet. Take Marshal Toker with you and meet with Duke Westin immediately. Assure him I'm taking the threat to our shores very seriously and will arrive with more troops as soon as practicable."

Jathez knew a dismissal when he heard one. "Westin and I are old friends. I'm sure he's confident you'll bring the help he needs."

After he'd left, the king looked to Becca and motioned toward the exit with his chin. Becca understood and immediately bowed herself out of the tent. He dismissed Nashotah with more diplomacy. "Thank you for coming to help, Nashotah, and please convey my thanks to Bodaway once more when you see him again."

Nashotah's eyes had narrowed at the king's peremptory dismissal of her lover, but this wasn't the time to discuss the matter. Her reply was somewhat cold and reserved. "There is much our two cultures can learn from one another. I'll be sure to pass along your message to my

Chief." Nodding to Bree, the healer let herself out of the tent, leaving Bree and a somewhat confused king alone in the tent.

The subtleties of dealing with women had always perplexed him, and now was no exception. "Did I say something wrong?"

Bree smiled slightly. "I don't think she appreciated the peremptory way you dismissed Becca." She watched him go from somewhat confused to completely at a loss.

"Why would she care how I dismiss one of my subjects?"

Garan groaned behind her and Bree once more chose to ignore him. "There's no reason for you to have known, but Becca and Nashotah have been lovers for quite a while."

"Lovers? An Anacafrian subject and a Shona healer?"

"According to Becca, Nashotah is now much more than simply a healer. Apparently, she recently succeeded Taklishim's wife as leader of the tribes. In the Shona culture, she's almost as revered as he is now."

Leopold barely kept his anger in check as he questioned his cousin. "And neither of you thought that was something I should know?"

"I'm sorry, Leo. Becca just told me last night when I went to check on the wounded in the healer's tent. I haven't had a chance to speak with you about it until now."

He rubbed his eyes with the fingers of both hands. "And I've been treating her as a healer when I should have been according her the same honor as a fellow monarch."

"No. The Shona have chiefs whom they respect and honor...and usually fear. Even though Taklishim is revered as a shaman, they don't understand the concept of a divine monarchy. As you've seen these past few days, our culture and beliefs are just as foreign to them as theirs is to us. Like Nashotah said, we have a lot we can learn from each other."

Leopold studied her a moment, trying to translate the nuances she was attempting to convey. "Well, we can discuss this at length some other time. For now, I'll expect you to join me in King's City within the half-fortnight. I'm sure Arabetha will have your rooms prepared for you, and if I know my wife, she'll be expecting to honor you with a formal dinner while you're our guest."

There was nothing Bree hated more than formal state dinners. As a young child, her parents shoved her into detested corsets and dresses, insisting she attend at least the more prestigious dinners held by King Prius and Queen Celeste. At the time, she'd thought they wanted her to put into practice the manners she'd been taught in the nursery, and later, she'd assumed they'd wanted her to be seen moving about among the social elite. It was only later, when she'd grown to understand the brutality of her uncle's reign, that she'd realized her parents had been trying to keep their heads on their shoulders by attending at the behest of the king.

After her parents had passed, she'd had the onerous duty of cleaning out her father's credenza, a monstrosity he'd kept in his den. Twenty or more cubby holes lined the interior, stuffed to the gills with papers, poems and musings her father thought might be important someday. The poems and musings she'd kept—her father had actually been a fair poet in his day—but she'd discarded almost everything else.

Tucked deep into the far reaches of one of those compartments she'd discovered a packet of invitations from King Prius, each requesting his brother's presence and commanding that he appear "with your family in its entirety." After she'd discovered the royal missives, all of the family battles over her refusal to attend the royal engagements suddenly made perfect sense.

Her musings took no more than a few seconds, and Bree looked up at Leopold, who was expecting her to complain bitterly about having to attend one of Arabetha's dinners. "You know, your mother, Queen Celeste, knew how much I detested those events. On one particular evening, she was dressed in a beautiful burgundy ball gown with puffed, billowy sleeves. I remember we were standing at a table, just the two of us, and we both reached for the same appetizer. The sleeve of her dress pulled back slightly, and I saw a black and red bruise on her forearm in the shape of a hand. I can still see those dark red fingers wrapping around her delicate wrist. I froze, and she elegantly pulled down her sleeve."

Bree watched as the color rose in her cousin's cheeks, and then continued her story. "She took my chin in her hand and bent close until she was sure she had my undivided attention. She said, 'I know how much you hate these events, but it is so very important that you attend.'"

Lost in the memory, Bree rubbed her forearm where she'd seen the queen's bruise so many years before. "I was around nine or ten, and although I didn't fully understand her meaning, I knew it had something to do with your father, and from that night on, I never argued with my parents about attending one of his events again."

Bree watched Leopold's jaw clench and unclench as he chose a piece of fruit from the bowl on the table.

He remained quiet for some time as he polished an apple on the quilted sleeve of his gambeson. He seemed to be lost in his own memories, and she waited patiently until he was ready to speak.

He finally gathered his thoughts and looked up at her. "I've never spoken about what I'm going to tell you to anyone before, but I think it's important for you to know more than you already do about my father. You and I spent a lot of time together as children, and I know you were privy to much of what went on after the throne room had been emptied and all the political posturing was left on the other side of the heavy oaken doors." He paused, shaking his head slightly as he remembered things that he'd tried to bury in the darker recesses of his mind. "Do you remember my Uncle Raniard, my mother's brother? You might not, we were both pretty young."

Bree nodded. "I remember because it was so awful the way he died trying to catch his young son who'd crawled out onto a ledge in their tower apartments. When I was a child, I used to imagine what it must have been like for them both as they fell the three stories knowing they were going to die."

"That son? Guillan was his name. He was my cousin on my mother's side and my playmate. We were about four, I think. He'd come down with some kind of illness, and even though my father had commanded Raniard to attend one of those political dinners with his entire family, Raniard left Guillan at home with his nurse."

Leo turned and set the apple back in the bowl. "My Uncle Raniard 'tried to save his son' the next day, while my father and I watched." He looked up and held Bree's gaze. "My father's guards threw Raniard and Guillan to their deaths because Raniard had dared disobey his command to bring his son to the dinner the night before. He brought me along to watch and learn, as he was so fond of saying. So, Bree, any time you don't want to attend one of Arabetha's formal dinners, I have absolutely no problem with that."

Appalled at the horrors her cousin must have witnessed as a child, Bree put a hand on his arm. "I'd come, if only to honor my king, who, thankfully, is not his father's son." She held up a finger in his face. "But I refuse to wear a corset or a dress."

He laughed at that. Holding open the tent flap, he waved her out. "You will scandalize my aristocratic guests... yet again."

Bree nodded as she ducked outside. "I should hope so."

CHAPTER 10

They stepped into the bright morning sun where Kaiti waited impatiently by the stone ring of a cold campfire. When she saw Bree, she dropped the stick she was holding and ran over, her expression serious and disturbed. The little girl ignored Leopold and Bree took her by her shoulders and made her face the king. "You need to bow good morning to your king."

Bree mimed bowing, and Kaiti immediately understood her mistake. Gathering herself, she faced Leopold and bowed formally as she'd been taught. "Good Morrrn...ing." She pronounced the words as well as she could, but the nuances of the Anacafrian language still eluded her.

The king smiled down at her. "Good morning to you as well. I see you're finally learning some Anacafrian."

The only words Kaiti understood were 'good morning' and 'Anacafrian.' She glanced over to her mother, whose proud expression told her she'd done well. With the formalities over, Kaiti quickly pointed to the edge of the encampment where Jathez had taken the six traitors.

Several soldiers were stringing ropes over some tree branches, and

Bree misunderstood the source of Kaiti's apprehension. "Yes, those men are going to hang for what they did yesterday."

Kaiti couldn't tell if her mother understood what she was seeing. She only knew the Shona words for the black guides she saw hovering around the six men. They hadn't attacked anyone yet, and Kaiti wondered if it was because the men had their hands tied behind their backs and weren't able to fight. She didn't know if the humans had to fight in order for the black guides to attack, and there were a lot of people gathering to watch the hangings.

Two of the black shadows turned her way.

Her heart skipped a beat as they detached themselves from their hosts and flew toward her face before breaking off at the last second to fly in circles around King Leopold. They made several passes, darting over and under him before returning to the trees where their hosts stood awaiting the king's judgment.

After they landed, Kaiti grabbed Bree's tunic with both fists. "Shimaa! The black guides!"

Still thinking Kaiti was upset about the men being hung, she gently pried the little girl's fingers off and knelt down in front of her. "I know it's hard to understand, and I wish you knew enough Anacafrian to know what I'm telling you, but those men are traitors who have been sentenced to die by the king."

The time had come for Leopold to join Jathez, but as he watched Kaiti getting so upset, he thought it might be better if she didn't attend. "Bree, call your healer and have her take the child somewhere else while we attend the hanging."

Neither Becca nor Nashotah were nearby, but Bree spotted Liris as she helped some soldiers dismantle one of the larger tents. "Liris. Could you come here a minute?"

Liris glanced in her direction, and then handed her end of the tent to one of the soldiers. She walked over, bowed to the king and faced Bree. "Your Grace?"

"Would you take Kaiti somewhere, so she doesn't have to see the hangings?"

"Of course."

When Bree and the king began walking to the edge of the encampment, Kaiti ran after them. "Shimaa!"

Liris hurried after her and took Kaiti by the shoulders, holding her back. "You stay with me, Little One. Let's go over here and help take down this tent." She tried to steer Kaiti in the other direction, but Kaiti pulled out of her arms, and, after quickly glancing at Bree's retreating back, turned and ran at a full sprint across the camp and into Taklishim's tent.

"Damn." Liris took off after her but stopped short when she found herself staring into Tisneé's questioning face.

He was at his customary guard position outside Taklishim's tent and was unsure why this woman was chasing the Spirit Child, who'd just run past him into the tent. He casually fingered the battleax hanging at his side, a gesture that didn't go unnoticed.

Liris well remembered how deadly Tisneé had been with that particular weapon. She glanced toward Bree and the king who were nearing the place of execution. An involuntary shudder ran through her as she remembered how close she and her men had come to hanging from a tree themselves.

She shrugged as she looked back at the warrior. "Well, the child can't see anything from in there, so I guess it won't hurt to leave her." Turning her back to the opening, she took up a guard position next to Tisneé and waited.

When Kaiti ran into the tent, both Taklishim and Ebi were asleep. Knowing she didn't want to wake Taklishim, she knelt next to Ebi and gently shook her. When the Badger didn't respond, she leaned down and smelled the Guide's breath. Sure enough, the smell of Becca's potions was strong and Kaiti knew she'd get no help from that quarter.

The king's voice carried across the encampment as he began his judgment.

Panic tightened Kaiti's chest until she could barely breath. She whispered quietly into the morning air. "Denabi, I need help!" When Denabi didn't appear right away, the tightness increased. She waited a few heartbeats, hoping the familiar shape of the Black Panther would emerge from the other realms. "Denabi, please! I need to tell you something."

She glanced over at Taklishim and jumped when she saw Acoma lying quietly next to the shaman, watching her.

He slowly blinked but said nothing.

Talking to Acoma frightened her more than speaking with Taklishim. The Shona treated him with the deference they showed Aevala, and Kaiti wasn't sure how to, or if, she should approach him.

They stared at each other for a long moment before Kaiti decided she'd rather go find Becca, and by extension, Garan.

When she turned to go, Acoma spoke. *What disturbs you, Spirit Child?*

She froze, not daring to move. Her mind locked up along with her feet, and she stood poised with one foot in front of the other, a runner waiting for the order to run.

Acoma casually padded to the opening of the tent. He sat so that he blocked her only exit. He saw panic sweep across her face, and he lay down so as not to intimidate her any further. *You are free to leave if you wish, but I would know what troubles you. You are not easily upset, and if I can, I will help.*

The king's voice sounded louder now, and Kaiti knew she had to act. Swallowing her fear, she spoke quietly, making sure to keep her eyes trained on the ground at his feet. "There are black guides on the men who are going to hang. I think the guides threatened the king, but I can't tell if they can do anything while the men have their hands tied behind their backs. I don't know what to do."

Acoma immediately stood. *Come.* He strode out of the tent and trotted toward the executions.

When Kaiti ducked out of the tent and attempted to follow, Liris grabbed her arm. "Here now, your mother said you're supposed to stay away from all that. I'm sorry, but I can't let you go."

Kaiti didn't understand the words and began to struggle against the strong hands holding her back.

Tisneé's callused hand gripped Liris' arm, and she looked over her shoulder, unsure of her next move. "The Duchess told me to keep her away from the hangings."

They were at an impasse, neither soldier nor warrior willing to back down.

As a Mapînéh Fox, Acoma wasn't one of the larger Spirit Guides, but Kaiti still jumped when he barked out a commanding growl. *We don't have time for this!*

Legan, the Fisher who was Liris' Guide, immediately appeared next to the Fox, his head tilted toward him as though awaiting instructions.

Acoma indicated Liris with a quick movement of his head. *Tell her the child needs to come with me.*

Liris immediately released Kaiti's arm. "You could have told me that yourself."

Acoma closed his eyes slightly. *I forgot you were graced with the Aevalian Gift. All of you, follow me.*

Everyone except Tisneé followed Acoma through the camp.

Before they'd gotten very far, Denabi appeared. *I heard you calling, Kitten, but I couldn't come right away. I asked Acoma to stand in for me. Is there a problem?* Denabi paced next to Kaiti, scanning the area around them for trouble.

Garan also appeared, as did several other Guides whom Kaiti didn't recognize.

Acoma answered for her. *The child has seen black guides on the men who are to be hanged. She believes they are possibly a threat to the king.*

At that moment, the largest Mountain Goat Kaiti had ever seen appeared next to King Leopold.

Darius' Guide, the Silvermoor Leopard Brékin, appeared simultaneously with the Goat.

By this time, the condemned men were standing on the hind quarters of six enormous cart horses, each of them with their hands bound tightly behind their backs and a rope tied around their necks.

Kaiti stood to the side, nervously watching as all of the Guides surrounded the king and his son.

Bree stood slightly in front of Leopold and didn't notice the Guides until Acoma calmly walked over to the horses and sat staring at the condemned men. When she glanced back and noticed several battle-ready Guides surrounding both Leopold and Darius, she rested a hand on one of her throwing knives.

Denabi's shoulders tensed and her tail begin to twitch.

When Bree saw that Kaiti had joined them as well, she sent an angry glare at Liris, who pursed her lips and stepped in front of the child. She rested her hand on the hilt of her shortsword.

Just as the king nodded to Jathez, Kaiti watched the black guides change into the forms of jackals.

They bared their teeth and dove directly at Darius.

Her voice rose several octaves as she screamed, "Darius!"

Surprised, both the king and the prince turned toward her.

Kalsik whipped his sword from its scabbard and immediately scanned their surroundings.

All of the Spirit Guides converged around the young prince, swinging their heads from side-to-side with teeth snapping in an attempt to stop their invisible foe.

Denabi blindly leapt in front of Darius, only to have a jackal drive her back into the boy with such force he fell backward into the dirt.

Unsure what had happened, Kalsik moved to stand over him, sword in one hand, a dirk in the other. His eyes flew this way and that searching for an enemy to battle.

A second jackal lunged toward Darius' head.

Not able to give warning in time, Katie threw herself forward and grabbed the beast by its shoulders. She clung to the fur until Brékin guessed the position of the animal and grabbed it by its throat, tearing out the jugular.

Kaiti fell to the ground on top of the creature, only to be hauled up by Liris who wrapped her arms around the girl and knelt over her, covering her body with her own.

Acoma bellowed, *Hang them! Now!*

Bree reacted instantly. "Whip the horses!"

Without hesitation, six soldiers stepped forward and whipped the horses out from under the prisoners.

The horses lurched forward, and the men fell with enough force to instantly snap their necks.

Seconds before reaching the prince, the remaining black guides screamed. One-by-one, as each man died, the jackals dissipated into formless wisps of smoke that rose slowly and disappeared into the cool morning air.

Shaken, Kaiti took a second to gather her wits before letting the

Guides know the Teivaiedin were gone. "The men are dead, so the jackals are gone."

Immediately after she spoke, the distinctive scream of an enraged Teivaiedin echoed from the highest bluffs in the hills behind the encampment.

Kaiti whipped her head around, scanning the crags of the rocks for any sign of evil.

Bree came and motioned for Liris to get off the girl. When Kaiti stood, Bree laid her arm across her shoulders, carefully searching the hillside that had caught and held the child's attention.

Kaiti didn't see anything, so she turned and faced the king.

Shocked and confused, the king's blank expression alternated between Kaiti and his son.

Kaiti leaned into Bree, relieved when Becca and Nashotah came running from the camp, weapons ready for a fight. When they arrived, she explained exactly what she'd seen.

From up on the mountainside, a lone figure watched as people gathered around the prince and the girl. He saw Kalsik sheath his sword and snarled at the sight of the king who'd deposed him. His eyes slid to the six men who'd served him so faithfully. As their bodies swayed at the end of their ropes, the bitterness he'd felt at their deaths increased tenfold. Jeffries' lip curled as his gaze once more rested on Leopold and his son. He spoke slowly, a feral snarl emphasizing each word. "Your life for their lives. Your blood for their blood. This I do swear and will uphold for as long as there is breath in my body."

ALSO BY ALISON NAOMI HOLT

Mystery

Credo's Hope - Alex Wolfe Mysteries Book 1

Credo's Legacy – Alex Wolfe Mysteries Book 2

Credo's Fire – Alex Wolfe Mysteries Book 3

Credo's Bones - Alex Wolfe Mysteries Book 4

Credo's Betrayal - Alex Wolfe Mysteries Book 5

Credo's Honor - Alex Wolfe Mysteries Book 6

Credo's Bandidos - Alex Wolfe Mysteries Book 7

Fantasy Fiction

The Spirit Child – The Seven Realms of Ar'rothi Bk 1

Duchess Rising – The Seven Realms of Ar'rothi Bk 2

Duchess Rampant- The Seven Realms of Ar'rothi Bk 3

Spyder's Web - The Seven Realms of Ar'rothi Bk 4

Mage of Merigor

Psychological Thriller

The Door at the Top of the Stairs

ABOUT THE AUTHOR

"A good book is an event in my life." – Stendhal

Alison, who grew up listening to her parents reading her the most wonderful books full of adventure, heroes, ducks and puppy dogs, promotes reading wherever she goes and believes literacy is the key to changing the world for the better.

In her writing, she follows Heinlein's Rules, the first rule being *You Must Write.* To that end, she writes in several genres simply because she enjoys the great variety of characters and settings her over-active fantasy life creates. There's nothing better for her then when a character looks over their shoulder, crooks a finger for her to follow and heads off on an adventure. From medieval castles to a horse farm in Virginia to the police beat in Tucson, Arizona, her characters live exciting lives and she's happy enough to follow them around and report on what she sees.

She has published nine fiction novels and one screenplay. Her first novel, The Door at the Top of the Stairs, is a psychological suspense, which she's also adapted as a screenplay. The Screenplay advanced to the Second Round of the Austin Film Festival Screenplay & Teleplay

Competition, making it to the top 15% of the 6,764 entries. The screenplay also made the quarter finalist list in the Cynosure Screen-writing awards.

Alison's previous life as a cop gave her a bizarre sense of humor, a realistic look at life, and an insatiable desire to live life to the fullest. She loves all horses & hounds and some humans...

For more information:
https://alisonholtbooks.com

GLOSSARY

GLOSSARY

Acoma (uh-KOH-muh): Mapînéh Fox from Peritia, the 6th Realm – Guide for Taklishim

Adené (ah-din-AY): (*Minet*) Shona. Healer for Dahana's tribe

Aecheron (AY-shur-on): Underworld ruled by Morgrad

Aeval (EYE-vol): Goddess of Aevalia, the 1st Realm – Creator of the Spirit Guides

Aevalian Gifts (eye-VOL-yan): A rare gift from the goddess Aeval that allows the

person to see and hear all Spirit Guides

Aikyla (ay-Key-la): Doe from Tane'iel, 2nd Realm of Ar'rothi - Guide for Sarai

Alaqúua (ah-LAH-koo-ah) Shona term for same sex couples

Anacafria (ana-CA-free-uh) A kingdom in the 1st Realm of Aevalia

Anaya (uhn-EYE-ya): Ancient Shona Philosopher

Andrin Magnus Estia: Estian noble who serves with Liris

Arabetha: (air-a-BEETH-uh) Queen of Anacafria

Arnis: Sentry, Guide: Stepit Eagle, Torsal

Ashton Fork: Small town in the duchy of Danforth.

Aysha (AY-shah): Meerkat from Peritia, 6ᵗʰ Realm Ar'rothi – Guide for Kayah

Azeel: Shengali Hawk. Spirit Guide for Tisneé

Banon: Congreve, Peer of the Realm, substitute father to Leopold

Bendi: 3ʳᵈ Realm of Ar'rothi

Bendith: God of Bendi, the 3ʳᵈ Realm Ar'rothi

Bodaway (BO-duh-way): (*Hekla*) Shona. Chief of a Shona Tribe

Book of Opprobrium: Record of people who have been disgraced

Breah (BRAY-uh): Shona. Taima's daughter and Tisneé and Seshawah's mother

Brékin: (Breh-kin): Silvermoor Leopard from Peritia – Spirit Guide for Darius

Cameron: Squire to Jathez

Cafria (CA-free-yuh): Capital of Anacafria. Also known as King's City

Cascadian Sea: Northeastern sea

Celest: Prius' wife, Queen during his reign.

Chethan (CHEE-thahn): Chief of Shona tribe

Cole, Bennet: Citizen of Organdy traveling to Ashton Fork with his wife and daughter.

Cole, Alilya (ah-LIL-ya): Citizen of Organdy. Bennet Cole's wife

Cole, Cylia (SIL-yuh): Citizen of Organdy. Daughter of Bennet and Alilya Cole

Conn: Black Ferret from Tane'iel, the 2ⁿᵈ Realm of Ar'rothi - Guide for Nolgee

Dado (DAY-doh) Derogatory slang for someone with both Shona and Anacafrian blood

Dahana (duh-HAH-nuh): (Dyénu) Chief of a Shona tribe

Dalney, Zer (Zehr): Anacafrian. Citizen of Ashton Fork

Danforth: Duchy in Anacafria. Bree Makena is the Duchess of Danforth

Darius: Crown Prince of Anacafria

Darma (DAR-muh): Shona warrior in Dahana's tribe

Deerhaven: Town in Southeast Danforth

Deelan: Trapper in Anacafria

Denabi (Deh-NOB-ee) Black Panther from Perit, the 6th Realm Ar'rothi – Guide for Kaiti

Desdamea: Queen of Organdy: Standard: a yellow shield with serpents spiraling up two crossed swords

Dyénu (d'eye-EN-oo): Shengali Hawk from Bendi, the 3rd Realm of Ar'rothi - Guide for Dahana

Eavan: King Leopold's squire

Ebi (EH-bee): Badger from Fandrin, the 4th Realm of Ar'rothi - Guide for Bree Makena

Ellsworth, Mosvor: Steward for the Duchess Bree Makena in Danforth

Estia: Kingdom to the East of Anacafria – Symbol - Cormorant

Estian Wars: War fought when Bree was in her late teens

Esul: Nashotah's bay horse

Fand: God of Fandrin, the 4th Realm of Ar'rothi

Fletcher, Burld: Woodsman in Danforth

Fraval Bread: Bread with dried fruit

Garan (GAH-ren): White Wolf from Bendi, the 3rd Realm of Ar'rothi – Guide for Becca Solárin

Gariale: (Gah-rhe-ale) Teyvardian Mountain Goat – Spirit Guide for King Leopold

Gitli (GIT-lee): (*Seakla*) Shona warrior in Dahana's tribe

Hayden: Soldier with hooked nose, friend of Becca's

Hecla (HEH-claw): Golden Civet from Bendi, the 3rd Realm of Ar'rothi – Guide for Bodaway

Hofni (HOF-nee): Shona warrior in Bodaway's tribe

Horay, Mreth (mer-ETH): Trapper

Hona (HOE-nuh): Deer from Tane'iel, the 2nd Realm of Ar'rothi - Guide for Jivin

Hreth (Reth): Mountain Lion from Tane'iel, the 2nd Realm of Ar'rothi - Guide for Nugén

Humphries: Baron of Tessarod

Inea (i-NAY-uh): Shona warrior in Dahana's tribe. Gitli's daughter

Jathez (Jaythez): Lord Commander of the Imperial Guard

Jeffries, Merand: Deposed Baron of Guildenhall

Jivin (JIH-vin): (*Hona*) Shona Healer in Bodaway's tribe, apprenticed to Nashotah.

Kalian (KAHL-yan): Black Panther from Lamina, 5th Realm of Ar'rothi - Guide for Nashotah

Kalsik: Bree's cousin, son of Gregrin. Also, Darius' bodyguard and a weapons instructor

Kayah (KAH-ya): (*Aysha*) Shona wise woman from Chethan's tribe. Taklishim's wife

Kem: Great Horned Owl from Tane'iel, the 2nd Realm of Ar'rothi - Guide for Timur

Kemin (KEH-min): Shona warrior from Dahana's tribe. Gitli's brother

Kirin: Cook for Bree

Kon: An Anacafrian sub-commander from Thadon.

Kotólo (ko-TOLE-oh): Ancient Shona philosopher

Lamin (LAH-min): God of Lamina, the 5th Realm of Ar'rothi

Leez: One of Liris' men from Estia. An archer and fletcher with "C" branded on his face

Legan (Lehg-in) A Fisher. Spirit Guide to Liris

Leopold: King of Anacafria

Lidup: King of Estia

Lisrin: Royal messenger

Loneh (LOH-neh): Shona warrior in Dahana's tribe. Tisnee's brother who kidnapped Kaiti as a baby

Lorek: Sub-commander under Marshal Toker

Marok: Assigned to the Royal Messenger Service

Makena, Bree: (*Ebi*) Duchess of Danforth.

Makena, Kaiti: (*Denabi*) The Spirit Child. Adopted daughter of Bree Makena

Malygar Forest (MAL-i-gar): Forest in Tane'iel, the 2nd Realm of Ar'rothi

Mekéneh (Meh-KEN-eh): (*Li*) Shona warrior in Dahana's tribe and son of Adené

Minet (min-ET): Cricket from Fandrin, the 4th Realm of Ar'rothi - Guide for Adené

Miri: Kaiti's little white mare with a grey mane and tail

Miri: Guide who accompanies Aevala on all of her travels through the Realms

Morgrad: God of the Underworld

Muda (MOO-duh): (*Slokum*) Shona. Dahana's son.

Nashotah (nuh-SHOW-tuh): (*Kalian*) Shona healer and warrior in Bodaway's tribe

Nolgee (NOL-geh-eh): (*Conn*) Shona warrior in Chethan's tribe. Taklishim's grandson

Nucat (new-KOHT): Coyote from Tane'iel, the 2nd Realm of Ar'rothi. Guide for St'ena

Nugén (new-GHEN): (*Hreth*) Shona warrior in Bodaway's tribe

Nul (Nool): (*T'es*) Shona warrior in Bodaway's tribe

Organdy: Kingdom to the north and east of Anacafria. Colors yellow and red

Orinshire: Capital city of the duchy of Danforth

Outer Territories: Westernmost portion of Anacafria. Includes the Silvermoor Steppes

in the duchy of Danforth and the Gilded Forest in the duchy of Thadon

Perit (PEHR-it): God of Peritia, the 6th Realm of Ar'rothi

Peritia (pehr-EE-shuh) 6th Realm of Ar'rothi

Peshár (PESH-ar): Sacred Shona word for the Spirit Guides

Peshárîn (PESH-ar-in) Shona word for "The bond that goes beyond." This is a rare bond

between two beings whose destinies are so intertwined their bond spans several lifetimes and reaches into the farthest Realms

Pogan (POG-an): (*Siklan*) Shona warrior from Dahana's tribe

Pries (PREE-us): Previous king of Anacafria. King Leopold's father

Príusin (PREE-us-in): Legendary Shona Spirit Guide

Queen's Battalions: All-women battalion of Anacafrian soldiers commanded by the

Queen.

R'ardas, Timur (ra-AR-dus): Deceased wife of Bree Makena, Duchess of Danforth

Ranr: (Ran-ur) Guard for Kaiti. A Chite who is Nordin's lover

Richond, Negril: Arms Master at Deerford

Régula: Legendary Shona Spirit Guide

Rhia'an (shi-uh-AN): Civet from Bendi, the 3rd Realm of Ar'rothi - Guide for Zia

Rocca Andresin: One of the King's bodyguards

Royal Archers: Elite group of Anacafrian archers known for their skills as sniper

assassins.

Ruthok: the commander of the fourth contingent of the Royal Archers

Sandresin, Kilrik: Marshal under Bree. Baron of Falconworth in Thadon

Saluri Skivvers: Specialized knife used by the Saber Assassins of Organdy

Sabers: Assassins from Organdy

Seakla (SEE-klah): Blue-Spotted Hawk from Tane'iel, the 2nd Realm of Ar'rothi.

Seshawah (seh-SHAW-wa): Shona member of Dahana's tribe. Taima's granddaughter.

Shloe (shl-OH-eh): Shona. Taklishim's daughter.

Shirin: Commander under Marshal Toker

Silvermoor Steppes: Western edge of Danforth. The best horses in Anacafria are bred in the Steppes

St'ena (st-EHN-uh): (*Nucat*) Shona warrior in Dahana's tribe

Solárin, Becca: Anacafrian healer who lives and works with the Shona

Taima (TY-muh): Shona warrior in Bodaway's tribe

Taklishim (TOK-lih-sheem): (*Acoma*) Revered shaman, warrior and elder of the Shona

Tane: God of Tane'iel, the 2nd Realm of Ar'rothi

Teivaiedin (tay-VY-uh-din): Black Spirit Guides from Morgrad's Realm

Tisneé (Tis-nay-AY): (*Azeel*) Shona warrior in Bodaway's tribe. Taima's grandson

Toker, Andris, Marshall: The Baron of Lakeland. Son of Duke Westin of Salth

Tupper Tane Inn: An Inn in Orinshire

Tsoe (ts-OH-ay): Shona warrior in Chethan's tribe and Nolgee's father

Verigo Liris Estia: Niece of the current Estian king - sworn to Leopold

Westin: Duke of Salth

Yoren: Bree's cousin, Daughter of Gregrin

Zerad, Gregrin: Duke of Deerford

Zia: (*Shia'an*) Shona member of Chethan's tribe. Nolgee's mother, Taklishim's daughter

Made in the USA
Monee, IL
12 March 2023

29683152R00105